POP QUIZ FROM THE PAGES OF
COMMON KNOWLEDGE

1. What was the next state to join the Union after the original thirteen?

2. Who said, "I have nothing to declare except my genius," on passing through New York Customs?

3. Who was the first United States president born in the twentieth century?

4. In what cities are these television sitcoms set?
   a) "Mork and Mindy"
   b) "Designing Women"
   c) "The Mary Tyler Moore Show"
   d) "Happy Days"

5. Can you name the Seven Deadly Sins? . . . How about the Seven Dwarfs?

Answers 1. Vermont 2. Oscar Wilde 3. John F. Kennedy 4. a) Boulder, b) Colorado; b) Atlanta, Georgia; c) Minneapolis, Minnesota; d) Milwaukee, Wisconsin 5. Pride, greed, lust, anger, gluttony, envy, sloth; Doc, Dopey, Sneezy, Happy, Grumpy, Bashful, Sleepy

COMMON KNOWLEDGE

Joe Elder

FAWCETT GOLD MEDAL • NEW YORK

To Jenni and Larry, with Love

A Fawcett Gold Medal Book
Published by Ballantine Books
Copyright © 1991 by Joseph Elder

Library of Congress Catalog Card Number: 90-93476

ISBN 0-449-14696-0

Manufactured in the United States of America

First Edition: March 1991

Contents

Introduction

"Greg Norman seems sure to be remembered as golf's Sisyphus," proclaimed the opening line of a recent *New York Times* sports story. Reading it, there was a certain satisfaction, I realized, in knowing that Sisyphus was that mythical Greek who, for all eternity, was condemned in Hades to push a boulder up a steep hill, only to have it roll down to the bottom each time he neared the top. Golfer Greg Norman had recently lost several tournaments on the last hole to opponents who reached the cup from off the green. Hence the metaphor of Norman as a latter-day Sisyphus, one who almost makes it but loses at the last moment.

Though the Sisyphus/Norman connection is but one small byte of our common cultural heritage, we all have access to a vast body of culture from highest to lowest brow, from *haute* to pop. There is a connective tissue to this cultural legacy, and that is what these *Common Knowledge* quizzes address. From history to rock-and-roll, from Shakespeare to sitcoms, from architecture to cuisine, from baseball to Broadway, from quotations to quasars, *Common Knowledge* embraces a wide range of cultural riches. Some of these quizzes deal with specific subjects like sports or literature, while others (those called Common Knowledge) are more generalized in nature.

Of course, to lack knowledge of these things is not to be stupid. One can be highly intelligent and ignorant at the same time. To possess these cultural treasures, however, and to be able to draw upon them in all areas of life, from reading the newspaper to watching a ballgame to attending the opera, is intrinsically important. Having this cross-cultural *stuff* immediately at hand may make one a whiz at "Jeopardy," but more important, it can lend life a richness and depth, a range of colors, emotional nuances, and intellectual satisfactions that would otherwise be lacking.

These questions are not about the pursuit of the trivial, nor do they cop out by calling for multiple-choice, yes-or-no, or true-or-false answers. There may be a few exceptions to that disclaimer, and even a couple of tricky curve balls that I couldn't resist tossing into the game, but for the most part, the *Common Knowledge* questions are designed as a direct test not of one's traditional I.Q. (intelligence quotient), which measures native brainpower, but rather of what I call one's C.Q., or culture quotient.

Keeping Score

With only one exception (see DOUBLE TROUBLE), each of the following quizzes consists of 25 questions, many of which have two, three, or four parts to them. Score a total of four points for each question answered completely and correctly, or a total 100 points for a perfectly scored quiz. If the question has four parts, score one point for each part; if it has two parts, score two points for each. If the question has three parts, score one point for each part answered correctly, or a full four points if all three parts are answered correctly.

Your C.Q. may be gauged by the following table:

Score	C.Q. Level
0–20	Kindergarten
21–40	Grade School
41–60	High School
61–80	College
81–100	Graduate School

One quiz alone, of course, cannot determine your definitive C.Q. To find that figure, take at least ten of the quizzes in *Common Knowledge* and average your scores.

May this prove a pleasant and enlightening task and leave you, unlike Sisyphus (or Greg Norman for that matter), a clear winner!

Common Knowledge
1

1. It happened outside a New York City apartment house on December 8, 1980. Who did what to whom?

2. Gloria Swanson, Joan Crawford, and Rita Hayworth all played this fallen woman in the movies. Name—
    a) the character they played
    b) the original story in which she appears
    c) the author of the story

3. What do Latour, Petrus, and Haut-Brion have in common?

4. Jacob Schick invented it in 1931. What is it?

5. Name the two seas that bound Denmark on the east and west.

6. If sheep gather in flocks, what are groups of the following creatures called?
    a) lions
    b) fish
    c) ants
    d) clams

7. What is dowsing?

8. *Great Balls of Fire* was a hit record for him as well as the title of a movie based on his life. Who is this durable rock-and-roll performer?

9. Name the composers whose symphonies bear these nicknames:
    a) *Resurrection*
    b) *Pastoral*
    c) *London*
    d) *Unfinished*

10. In mathematics, what is a prime number?

11. What is the difference between *malfeasance* and *malpractice*?

12. What do José Orozco, Diego Rivera, and Rufino Tamayo have in common?

13. What do these initials mean when they follow a person's name?
    a) S.J.
    b) M.P.
    c) D.D.
    d) J.P.

14. This popular French salad includes tunafish, anchovies, and black olives. What is it called?

15. *Plié*, *jeté* and *entrechat* are terms used in what activity?

16. "Shoot, if you must, this old gray head":
    a) Name the poem the line comes from
    b) Name the poet
    c) Quote the next line

17. These performers on the original "Mary Tyler Moore Show" all went on to star in other long-running TV series. Name those series:

  a) Ed Asner
  b) Gavin McLeod
  c) Valerie Harper
  d) Betty White

18. Distinguish among the terms a) *carnivore*, b) *herbivore*, and c) *omnivore*.

19. Who said, "I cannot and will not cut my conscience to fit this year's fashions"?

20. What do *Cav* and *Pag* mean to an opera lover?

21. "A Study in Scarlet" was the first story about this celebrated fictional character. Name a) the character and b) his creator.

22. Which of these words does *not* belong with the others, and why?

  a) assiduous
  b) tenacious
  c) persistent
  d) insouciant

23. In modern history, only two queens of England have had no successors to the throne who bore their given names. Who were they?

24. What is the source of the words, ". . . we mutually pledge to each other our lives, our fortunes, and our sacred honor"?

25. Who wrote these literary works?
   a) *Death in Venice*
   b) *Death Comes for the Archbishop*
   c) *Death of a Salesman*
   d) "The Death of Ivan Ilyich"

Score_____

COMMON KNOWLEDGE 1: ANSWERS

1. Mark David Chapman murdered John Lennon.
2. a) Sadie Thomson, b) "Rain," c) W. Somerset Maugham.
3. They are all wines from the Bordeaux region of France.
4. The electric razor.
5. The Baltic on the east, the North on the west.
6. a) pride, b) school, c) colony, d) bed.
7. Searching for underground water with a forked stick known as a dowsing or divining rod.
8. Jerry Lee Lewis.
9. a) Gustav Mahler, b) Ludwig von Beethoven, c) Ralph Vaughan Williams, d) Franz Schubert.
10. A number such as 3, 5, or 7 that is evenly divisible only by itself and the number 1.
11. Malfeasance is wrongdoing by a public servant. Malpractice is wrongdoing by a professional such as a lawyer or a doctor.
12. All are distinguished Mexican artists.
13. a) Society of Jesus, b) Member of Parliament, c) Doctor of Divinity, d) Justice of the Peace.
14. Salade Niçoise.
15. Ballet dancing.
16. a) "Barbara Frietschie," b) John Greenleaf Whittier, c) "But spare your country's flag, she said."

17. a) "Lou Grant," b) "The Love Boat," c) "Rhoda,"
d) "The Golden Girls."
18. a) a meat-eating animal, b) a plant-eating animal, c) an
animal that eats both.
19. Lillian Hellman.
20. The operas *Cavalleria Rusticana* by Pietro Mascagni and
Pagliacci by Ruggiero Leoncavallo, which are usually performed on the same program.
21. a) Sherlock Holmes, b) Arthur Conan Doyle.
22. The first three imply stick-to-it-iveness, the fourth, *insouciant*, a more carefree attitude.
23. Anne and Victoria.
24. The Declaration of Independence.
25. a) Thomas Mann, b) Willa Cather, c) Arthur Miller,
d) Leo Tolstoy.

Hit or Myth

1. These creatures were part human and part something else.
Name the something else:
    a) Minotaur
    b) centaur
    c) satyr
    d) Harpy

2. What mythic hero sought the Golden Fleece?

3. What city did Dido rule over?

4. Who slew the troll-monster Grendel?

5. What Celtic spirit was known for its unearthly wailing
when someone died?

6. Name the two-faced Roman god of doorways.

7. Which of the following is *not* one of the Twelve Labors
of Hercules:
    a) Slaying the Nemean lion
    b) Slaying the Minotaur

    c) Slaying the Hydra
    d) Slaying the Erymanthian boar

8. Connect these Greek deities (left) with their Roman
equivalents (right):

a) Ares	a) Jupiter
b) Hera	b) Mercury
c) Hermes	c) Mars
d) Zeus	d) Juno

9. The mortally wounded King Arthur was taken to this
earthly paradise. Name it.

10. Also known as the Old Man of the Sea, this god had the
ability to change his shape. Who was he?

11. Regarding the Gorgon Medusa—
    a) Why was it hard to kill her?
    b) Who succeeded in doing so?
    c) How did he do it?

12. What might a lycanthrope view in the mirror?

13. How many Muses were there?

14. Who was the god of thunder in Norse mythology?

15. Which of the following escapes did *not* occur in the *Odyssey?*
    a) from the Lotus-Eaters
    b) from the Sirens
    c) from Circe
    d) from the Furies

16. Raised by wolves, these twins founded a great city.
Name a) them and b) the city.

17. a) Who in history/legend "cut the Gordian Knot," and b) what does this expression mean today?

18. After what Norse god was our day Wednesday named?

19. a) Who was Odysseus's wife, and b) how did she hold off her suitors while waiting for her long-absent husband?

20. This king of Cyprus lent his name to a play by George Bernard Shaw, which in turn inspired a Broadway musical. Name a) the king/play and b) the musical.

21. Who was the Egyptian sun god?

22. Define these myth-inspired words and phrases:
     a) Pyrrhic victory
     b) procrustean
     c) between Scylla and Charybdis
     d) sword of Damocles

23. He tempted fate and fell to his death from a flying horse. Name a) the man and b) the horse.

24. King Mark's wife and his nephew became lovers in the Arthurian legends. a) Who were they, and b) who immortalized them in opera?

25. Whose face was it that "launched a thousand ships"?

Score_____

HIT OR MYTH: ANSWERS

1. a) bull, b) horse, c) goat, d) bird.
2. Jason.

3. Carthage.

4. Beowulf.

5. The banshee.

6. Janus.

7. b) Slaying of the Minotaur.

8. a) Mars, b) Juno, c) Mercury, d) Jupiter.

9. Avalon.

10. Proteus.

11. a) To look directly at her face turned one into stone;
b) Perseus killed her by c) viewing her reflection in his
shield and striking backward with his sword.

12. A werewolf.

13. Nine.

14. Thor.

15. d) from the Furies.

16. a) Romulus and Remus, b) Rome.

17. a) Alexander the Great. b) To cut the Gordian Knot
means to solve a seemingly difficult problem by swift and
bold action.

18. Odin, or Wotan.

19. a) Penelope b) told her suitors she would marry them
when she completed her weaving, but every night unwove
what she had done that day.

20. a) *Pygmalion,* b) *My Fair Lady.*

21. Ra.

22. a) A victory in which losses outweigh gains; b) forcing
conformity by cruel or violent means; c) facing equally
threatening alternatives, between a rock and a hard place; d)
a neverending threat hanging over one's head.

23. a) Bellerophon, b) Pegasus.

24. a) Tristram (Tristan) and Isolde, b) Richard Wagner.

25. Helen's.

Am I Blue?

1. Who wrote these "blue" songs?
    a) "Blue Moon"
    b) "Blue Skies"
    c) "St. Louis Blues"

2. What are so-called blue laws?

3. Where is the Blue Grotto located?

4. a) Who composed *Rhapsody in Blue*?
    b) Who conducted the first performance?
    c) Who performed the piano solo at that first performance?

5. High Society might consult this reference work. Name it.

6. Who is known as Old Blue Eyes?

7. What is the Bluegrass State?

8. What do bluebonnet, blue flag, and bluebell have in common?

9. If a woman is described as a bluestocking, she has—
   a) loose morals
   b) intellectual pretensions
   c) prudish attitudes
   d) varicose veins

10. Who is known as the Father of Bluegrass Music?

11. Alan Moorehead wrote a book about African exploration called *The Blue* _____.

12. Who painted *The Blue Boy*?

13. The Appalachian Trail winds through this rugged terrain. What is it?

14. Connect the following blue words with the appropriate occupations:
   a) blue chip   a) student
   b) blueprint   b) stockbroker
   c) blue book   c) engineer
   d) blue pencil   d) editor

15. A fairy-tale character inspired this opera by Bela Bartok. Name it.

16. Which side did the Blues fight on during the Civil War?

17. What folksinger/actor popularized the song "The Blue-Tailed Fly"?

18. Kings and aristocrats share this physiological property. What is it?

19. Match these "blue" movies with their stars:
  a) *The Blue Lagoon*   a) Elvis Presley
  b) *The Blue Angel*   b) Brooke Shields
  c) *Blue Hawaii*   c) Marlene Dietrich
  d) *The Blue Max*   d) George Peppard

20. Name a) the light blue properties and b) the dark blue properties on a Monopoly board.

21. What Walt Disney movie featured the song "Lavender Blue"?

22. In the poem "Little Boy Blue," where were the sheep and the cow?

23. Substitute a blue word or phrase for those in **boldface** below:
  Appearing a) **unexpectedly** at the restaurant, she noted that we hadn't met in a b) **very long time**, ordered the c) **featured dinner on the menu**, and talked d) **nonstop** while we ate.

24. Also known as a sulphur-bottom, it is the largest creature ever to have lived on Earth. Name it.

25. This Joseph Wambaugh novel became a TV miniseries. Name a) its title and b) the Emmy-winning actor who starred in it.

                                    Score_____

AM I BLUE?: ANSWERS

1. a) Richard Rodgers and Lorenz Hart, b) Irving Berlin, c) W. C. Handy.

2. Those prohibiting certain activities, particularly the sale and use of alcohol, on Sundays.

3. On the island of Capri, Italy.

4. a) George Gershwin, b) Paul Whiteman, c) George Gershwin.

5. *The Blue Book* (social register).

6. Frank Sinatra.

7. Kentucky.

8. They are all flowers.

9. b) intellectual pretensions.

10. Bill Monroe.

11. *Nile*.

12. Thomas Gainsborough.

13. The Blue Ridge Mountains.

14. a) stockbroker, b) engineer, c) student, d) editor.

15. *Bluebeard's Castle*.

16. The North or Union side.

17. Burl Ives.

18. Blue blood.

19. a) Brooke Shields, b) Marlene Dietrich, c) Elvis Presley, d) George Peppard.

20. a) Oriental, Vermont, and Connecticut avenues, b) Park Place and Boardwalk.

21. *Song of the South*.

22. "The sheep's in the meadow, the cow's in the corn."

23. a) out of the blue, b) blue moon, c) blue plate special, d) a blue streak.

24. The blue whale.

25. a) *The Blue Knight*, b) William Holden.

The Write Stuff

1. The following writers all used two initials in place of these first and middle names. What were their last names?
   a) Thomas Stearns
   b) Edward Estlin
   c) Henry Louis
   d) David Herbert

2. What more familiar name did William Sydney Porter write under?

3. How many lines are contained in a sonnet?

4. Robert Penn Warren was the first American to receive this honor, in 1986. What was it?

5. Match these novels with the wars they depict:

   a) *The Red Badge of Courage*   a) World War I
   b) *All Quite On the Western Front*   b) World War II
   c) *April Morning*   c) American Revolution
   d) *The Naked and the Dead*   d) Civil War

6. Historian Barbara W. Tuchman won two Pulitzer Prizes, for *Stillwell and the American Experience in China, 1911–45*, and for what other book?

7. This English author of *The Woman in White* is often considered the father of the modern detective novel. Name him.

8. Which of these plays was *not* written by Tennessee Williams?
  a) *Summer and Smoke*
  b) *Orpheus Descending*
  c) *The Skin of Our Teeth*
  d) *Night of the Iguana*

9. This form of poetry is written in three lines of five, seven, and five syllables respectively. What is it called?

10. Name the bestselling novelist who is sister to a star of TV's *Dynasty*.

11. A U.S. president-to-be won the Pulitzer Prize for biography. Name a) the president and b) his book.

12. This English statesman won the Nobel Prize for Literature. Who was he?

13. Match these mystery writers with their detective creations:
  a) S. S. Van Dine   a) Albert Campion
  b) P. D. James   b) Philo Vance
  c) Margery Allingham   c) Adam Dalgleish
  d) Dashiell Hammett   d) Sam Spade

14. What is the Newbery Medal awarded for?

15. Who wrote these "red" works of literature?
    a) *The Red and the Black*
    b) *The Mask of the Red Death*
    c) *The Thin Red Line*
    d) *The Red Pony*

16. For what book is Harriet Beecher Stowe best known?

17. Who wrote these "tales"?
    a) *A Tale of Two Cities*
    b) *Leatherstocking Tales*
    c) *Canterbury Tales*
    d) *Tales of the South Pacific*

18. a) What is a malapropism, and b) why is it so called?

19. Quote the first lines of the poems of which the following are the *second* lines, and name the poems and authors as well:
    a) "Bird thou never wert"
    b) "And one clear call for me"
    c) "Over many a quaint and curious volume of forgotten lore"
    d) "This coyness, Lady, were no crime"

20. *The Crucible* by playwright Arthur Miller is based on what episode in American history?

21. This most autobiographical of Charles Dickens's novels was also his favorite. Name it.

22. Her 1926 novel dealing with miscegenation was later adapted to the musical stage and the movies. Name a) the book and b) its author.

23. Each of the following authors wrote a literary work with the word "little" in the title. Name those works:
    a) Louisa May Alcott
    b) Antoine de Saint-Exupery
    c) Lillian Hellman
    d) Frances Hodgson Burnett

24. His daughter's memoir of her famous literary father was called *Home Before Dark*. Who was he?

25. This noted essayist also wrote the children's classics *Charlotte's Web* and *Stuart Little*. Name him.

Score_____

THE WRITE STUFF, ANSWERS

1. a) Eliot, b) Cummings, c) Mencken, d) Lawrence.
2. O. Henry.
3. Fourteen.
4. He was named the first American poet laureate.
5. a) Civil War, b) World War I, c) American Revolution, d) World War II.
6. *The Guns of August*.
7. Wilkie Collins
8. c) *The Skin of Our Teeth* was written by Thornton Wilder.
9. Haiku.
10. Jackie Collins.
11. a) John F. Kennedy, b) *Profiles in Courage*.
12. Winston Churchill.
13. a) Philo Vance, b) Adam Dalgleish, c) Albert Campion, d) Sam Spade.
14. Excellence in children's book writing.

15. a) Stendhal, b) Edgar Allan Poe, c) James Jones, d) John Steinbeck.

16. *Uncle Tom's Cabin*.

17. a) Charles Dickens, b) James Fenimore Cooper, c) Geoffrey Chaucer, d) James A. Michener.

18. a) A misuse of words to humorous effect, b) from the character Mrs. Malaprop in Richard Brinsley Sheridan's play *The Rivals*.

19. a) "Hail to thee, blithe spirit!" from "To A Skylark" by Percy Bysshe Shelley; b) "Sunset and evening star" from "Crossing the Bar" by Alfred, Lord Tennyson; c) "Once upon a midnight dreary, while I pondered, weak and weary" from "The Raven" by Edgar Allan Poe; d) "Had we but world enough, and time" from "To His Coy Mistress" by Andrew Marvell.

20. The Salem witch trials.

21. *David Copperfield*.

22. a) *Show Boat*, b) Edna Ferber.

23. a) *Little Women* (or *Little Men*), b) *The Little Prince*, c) *The Little Foxes*, d) *Little Lord Fauntleroy*.

24. John Cheever.

25. E. B. White.

Common Knowledge
2

1. A perfect game would score 300. In what sport?

2. Fill in the blanks: In the year a) _____, England was defeated by b) _____ the Conqueror at the Battle of c) _____.

3. Its lyrics taunted, "I bet you think this song is about you." Name a) the song and b) its singer/composer.

4. In what states are these national parks located?
   a) Mount Rainier
   b) Petrified Forest
   c) Grand Teton
   d) Acadia

5. *Cirrus*, *cumulus*, and *stratus*—what are they?

6. In what body of water are the Maldive and the Seychelles islands located?

7. Match these presidential memoirs with their authors:

a) *Keeping Faith*   a) Gerald Ford
b) *Mandate for*   b) Jimmy Carter
   Change   c) Dwight D. Eisen-
c) *A Time to Heal*   hower
d) *The Vantage Point*   d) Lyndon B. Johnson

8. What would one expect to find at Lick, Kitt, and Yerkes?

9. A 1939 letter to President Roosevelt helped to spur production of the first atomic bomb. Who wrote it?

10. In mathematics, what is a magic square?

11. To what Gilbert and Sullivan operas are these the subtitles?

a) *The Lass That Loved a Sailor*
b) *The Peer and the Peri*
c) *The Town of Titipu*
d) *The Slave of Duty*

12. This traditional French casserole of eggplant, zucchini, and tomatoes is called what?

13. What is the difference between a) libel and b) slander?

14. Who said, "England is a nation of shopkeepers"?

15. Other than being part of the United States, what do Alaska, Texas, Florida, Oklahoma, and West Virginia have in common?

16. During what historical conflict did the Reign of Terror take place?

17. Match these discoveries with their discoverers:
   a) bifocal lens   a) William Harvey
   b) penicillin   b) Benjamin Franklin
   c) vaccination   c) Edward Jenner
   d) circulation of blood   d) Alexander Fleming

18. The United States Air Force's Project Bluebook studied what phenomenon?

19. Name the Beatles' first movie.

20. What poets wrote these "songs"?
   a) "Song of Myself"
   b) "Songs of Innocence"
   c) "The Lovesong of J. Alfred Prufrock"
   d) "The Song of Hiawatha"

21. What was the first college established in what is now the United States?

22. What disastrous events occurred at these times in these places:
   a) 1937, Lakehurst, New Jersey
   b) 1956, off Nantucket Island
   c) 1967, Cape Kennedy, Florida
   d) 1984, Bhopal, India

23. What was the next state to join the Union after the original thirteen?

24. While Neil Armstrong and Edwin Aldrin walked on the moon, a third astronaut remained in moon orbit. Who was he?

25. "It is a far, far better thing that I do, than I have ever done. . . ." Identify—
  a) the character who speaks the line
  b) the novel in which it is spoken
  c) the author of the novel

Score_____

COMMON KNOWLEDGE 2: ANSWERS

1. Bowling.
2. a) 1066, b) William, c) Hastings.
3. a) "You're So Vain" by b) Carly Simon.
4. a) Washington, b) Arizona, c) Wyoming, d) Maine.
5. Clouds.
6. The Indian Ocean.
7. a) Jimmy Carter, b) Dwight D. Eisenhower, c) Gerald Ford, d) Lyndon B. Johnson.
8. Astronomers, or telescopes. They are observatories.
9. Albert Einstein.
10. A checkerboardlike square with numbers in each smaller square, the sum of which is the same in each row whether added horizontally, vertically, or diagonally.
11. a) *H.M.S. Pinafore*, b) *Iolanthe*, c) *The Mikado*, d) *The Pirates of Penzance*.
12. Ratatouille.
13. a) Libel defames another person through the written word, b) slander through the spoken word.
14. Napoleon Bonaparte.
15. They all have "panhandles."
16. The French Revolution.
17. a) Benjamin Franklin, b) Alexander Fleming, c) Edward Jenner, d) William Harvey.
18. Flying saucers.
19. *A Hard Day's Night*.

20. a) Walt Whitman, b) William Blake, c) T. S. Eliot, d) Henry Wadsworth Longfellow.

21. Harvard (1636).

22. a) The zeppelin *Hindenberg* burned and crashed, killing 36; b) the Italian liner *Andrea Dorea* sank, 52 dead; c) fire in a space capsule on the ground killed three astronauts; d) toxic gas from a Union Carbide plant killed more than 2,000.

23. Vermont.

24. Michael Collins.

25. a) Sydney Carton, b) *A Tale of Two Cities*, c) Charles Dickens.

Johnny-on-the-Spot

1. Provide the last names of these three-named Johns—
    a) John Singleton
    b) John James
    c) John Singer
and d) the one profession they had in common.

2. One John directed another in the movie *The Quiet Man* (among others). Name both a) director and b) star.

3. Four presidents of the United States were named John. Identify them.

4. What John was celebrated for his singing of Irish ballads as well as grand opera?

5. This bestselling John wrote *The Little Drummer Girl* among other works. Name him.

6. *King John* is among his least performed plays. Who is the playwright?

7. Identify these Johnnies by the songs they popularized:

a) "Take This Job and Shove It"
b) "The Little White Cloud That Cried"
c) "I Walk the Line"

8. What special distinction do John Dryden, John Masefield, and John Betjeman share?

9. Name a) the role and b) the film (later TV series) for which actor John Houseman achieved his greatest fame?

10. How many Popes (as of 1991) have been named just plain John?

11. Complete the names of these three-named Johns and connect them with their professions:

a) John Philip	a) cardinal
b) John Greenleaf	b) composer
c) John Henry	c) philosopher
d) John Stuart	d) poet

12. What is a johnny-jump-up?

13. Name the titular stars of the 1969 movie *John and Mary*.

14. Identify these "Johnny" films:
a) Jane Wyman won an Oscar for this one.
b) Dalton Trumbo directed, based on his own novel.
c) Walt Disney based it on a popular novel of the American Revolution.
d) Joan Crawford starred as a saloon keeper.

15. Who is the Johnny referred to in the title of the 1972 bestseller, *Johnny, We Hardly Knew Ye?*

16. This American folk hero was known as a "steel-drivin' man." Who was he?

17. Match these authors with their books:
  a) John Updike   a) *The Poorhouse*
  b) John Cheever   *Fair*
  c) John O'Hara   b) *From the Terrace*
  d) John Steinbeck   c) *Bullet Park*
                               d) *Winter of Our Dis-*
                               content

18. What was a Johnny Reb in U.S. history?

19. What does John Barleycorn personify?

20. What John was known as "Black Jack"?

21. Who was known as the Great Profile?

22. St. John had a brother who was also one of the Twelve Disciples. Name him.

23. What Johns wrote these immortal lines?
  a) "A thing of beauty is a joy forever"
  b) "They also serve who only stand and wait"
  c) "No man is an island"
  d) "I must go down to the seas again"

24. a) Who reputedly said, "Why don't you speak for yourself, John?" and b) whom was the speaker addressing?

25. Identify these Johnsons by their professions:
  a) an architect
  b) a boxer
  c) a lexicographer
  d) a president

Score_____

JOHNNY-ON-THE-SPOT: ANSWERS

1. a) Copley, b) Audubon, c) Sargent; d) all were artists.
2. a) John Ford, b) John Wayne.
3. a) John Adams, b) John Quincy Adams, c) John Tyler, d) John F. Kennedy.
4. John McCormack.
5. John Le Carre.
6. William Shakespeare.
7. a) Johnny Paycheck, b) Johnny Ray, c) Johnny Cash.
8. All were poet laureates of England.
9. a) Professor Charles W. Kingsfield, b) *The Paper Chase*.
10. Twenty-three.
11. a) Sousa, composer, b) Whittier, poet, c) Newman, cardinal, d) Mill, philosopher.
12. A flower.
13. Dustin Hoffman and Mia Farrow.
14. a) *Johnny Belinda*, b) *Johnny Got His Gun*, c) *Johnny Tremain*, d) *Johnny Guitar*.
15. President John F. Kennedy.
16. John Henry.
17. a) *The Poorhouse Fair*, b) *Bullet Park*, c) *From the Terrace*, d) *Winter of Our Discontent*.
18. A Confederate soldier in the Civil War.
19. Alcoholic beverages.
20. General John J. Pershing.
21. John Barrymore.
22. St. James.
23. a) Keats, b) Milton, c) Donne, d) Masefield.
24. a) Priscilla Mullens, b) John Alden.
25. a) Philip, b) Jack, c) Samuel, d) Andrew or Lyndon.

The Bottom Line

Name the title and author and quote the first line of the poems of which the following are *last lines*.

1. "And miles to go before I sleep."

2. "I shall but love thee better after death."

3. "Happy Christmas to all, and to all a good night!"

4. "And oh, 'tis true, 'tis true."

5. "I am the captain of my soul."

6. "Where ignorant armies clash by night."

7. "Fallen cold and dead."

8. "To strive, to seek, to find, and not to yield."

9. *"And the hunter home from the hill."*

10. "Till human voices wake us, and we drown."

11. "And all we need of hell."

12. "In her tomb by the sounding sea."

13. "And the mome raths outgrabe."

14. "And that has made all the difference."

15. "A little while, that in me sings no more."

16. "Rage, rage against the dying of the light."

17. "And hid his face amid a crowd of stars."

18. "Dare frame thy fearful symmetry?"

19. ". . .that is all / Ye know on earth, and all ye need to know."

20. "If Winter comes, can Spring be far behind?"

21. "All's right with the world!"

22. "He rose the morrow morn."

23. "But only God can make a tree."

24. "And dances with the daffodils."

25. "And—which is more—you'll be a man, my son!"

Score_____

THE BOTTOM LINE: ANSWERS

1. a) "Stopping by Woods On a Snowy Evening"
   b) Robert Frost
   c) "Whose woods these are I think I know"

2. a) *Sonnets from the Portuguese*, Sonnet 43
   b) Elizabeth Barrett Browning
   c) "How do I love thee? Let me count the ways"
3. a) "A Visit from St. Nicholas"
   b) Clement C. Moore
   c) " 'Twas the night before Christmas, when all through the house"
4. a) "When I was One-and-Twenty"
   b) A. E. Housman
   c) "When I was one-and-twenty"
5. a) "Invictus"
   b) William Ernest Henley
   c) "Out of the night that covers me"
6. a) "Dover Beach"
   b) Matthew Arnold
   c) "The sea is calm to-night"
7. a) "O Captain! My Captain!"
   b) Walt Whitman
   c) "O Captain! my Captain! Our fearful trip is done"
8. a) Ulysses
   b) Alfred, Lord Tennyson
   c) "It little profits that an idle king"
9. a) "Requiem"
   b) Robert Louis Stevenson
   c) "Under the wide and starry sky"
10. a) "The Love Song of J. Alfred Prufrock"
    b) T. S. Eliot
    c) "Let us go then, you and I"
11. a) "My Life Closed Twice . . ."
    b) Emily Dickinson
    c) "My life closed twice before its close"
12. a) "Annabel Lee"
    b) Edgar Allan Poe
    c) "It was many and many a year ago"
13. a) "Jabberwocky"
    b) Lewis Carroll

c) "Twas brillig, and the slithy toves"
14. a) "The Road Not Taken"
    b) Robert Frost
    c) "Two roads diverged in a yellow wood"
15. a) "What Lips My Lips Have Kissed"
    b) Edna St. Vincent Millay
    c) "What lips my lips have kissed, and where, and why"
16. a) "Do Not Go Gentle Into That Good Night"
    b) Dylan Thomas
    c) "Do not go gentle into that good night"
17. a) "When You Are Old"
    b) William Butler Yeats
    c) "When you are old and grey and full of sleep"
18. a) "The Tiger"
    b) William Blake
    c) "Tiger! Tiger! burning bright"
19. a) "Ode On a Grecian Urn"
    b) John Keats
    c) "Thou still unravished bride of quietness!"
20. a) Ode to the West Wind b) Percy Bysshe Shelley
    c) "O wild West Wind, thou breath of Autumn's being"
21. a) "Pippa's Song"
    b) Robert Browning
    c) "The year's at the spring"
22. a) "The Rime of the Ancient Mariner"
    b) Samuel Taylor Coleridge
    c) "It is an ancient Mariner"
23. a) "Trees"
    b) Joyce Kilmer
    c) "I think that I shall never see"
24. a) "Daffodils (or "I Wandered Lonely . . .")
    b) William Wordsworth
    c) "I wandered lonely as a cloud"
25. a) "If"
    b) Rudyard Kipling
    c) "If you can keep your head when all about you"

Hooray for Hollywood

1. Connect the characters in these movie titles:
   - a) *Sid and* —
   - b) *Melvyn and* —
   - c) *Harold and* —
   - d) *Harry and* —

   - a) *Maude*
   - b) *Howard*
   - c) *Nancy*
   - d) *Tonto*

2. Who played Agatha Christie's detective Hercule Poirot in a) *Murder On the Orient Express*, and in b) *Death On the Nile*?

3. Only one of the following movie musicals was based on a prior Broadway musical. Which one?
   - a) *Singin' In the Rain*
   - b) *Seven Brides for Seven Brothers*
   - c) *Li'l Abner*
   - d) *Mary Poppins*

4. What actress appeared both in Orson Welles's classic film *Citizen Kane* and in the soap opera *All My Children*?

5. Match these actresses with the Alfred Hitchcock movies in which they starred:

a) Kim Novak
b) Joan Fontaine
c) Doris Day
d) Tallulah Bankhead

a) *The Man Who Knew Too Much*
b) *Lifeboat*
c) *Vertigo*
d) *Suspicion*

6. Who directed the cult horror classic *Night of the Living Dead*?

7. Match these movies with the composers whose lives they depict:

a) *Song of Love*
b) *Song to Remember*
c) *Song Without End*

a) Frederic Chopin
b) Franz Liszt
c) Robert Schumann

8. This film won an Oscar for its star, who appeared in it for the first and only time with his daughter. Name a) the film, b) the father, and c) the daughter.

9. Katharine Hepburn won four Oscars, for *Morning Glory, Guess Who's Coming to Dinner?*, *On Golden Pond*, and for one other film. Name a) the fourth movie, and b) the female star with whom she shared the Oscar that year.

10. What actor played the "voice" of Darth Vader in the *Star Wars* movies?

11. Which of the following is a James Bond movie?
    a) *The Spy Who Came in From the Cold*
    b) *The Spy Who Loved Me*
    c) *The Spy With My Face*

12. Marlon Brando and Robert De Niro played the same character in two related movies. Name a) the character and b) the movies.

13. Connect these "lost" films with the issues they deal with:

a) *The Lost Weekend*   a) vampirism
b) *Lost In the Stars*   b) alcoholism
c) *The Lost Boys*   c) racism
d) *Lost in America*   d) escapism

14. What do the initials stand for in the film title *E.T.*?

15. Who wrote the novels on which the following films were based?

a) *The World According to Garp*
b) *Jaws*
c) *Dune*
d) *Death in Venice*

16. What country singers' lives inspired these movies?

a) *Coal Miner's Daughter*
b) *Sweet Dreams*
c) *Your Cheatin' Heart*

17. John Barrymore, Frederic March, and Spencer Tracy all starred in movies based on the same story. Name a) the story and b) its author.

18. What competitive activities are featured in these films?

a) *Breaking Away*
b) *Smile*
c) *The Competition*
d) *Hoosiers*

19. Match these "kids" with the actors who played them in the movies:

a) *The Flamingo Kid*   a) Ralph Macchio
b) *The Heartbreak Kid*   b) Eric Roberts
c) *The Karate Kid*   c) Charles Grodin
d) *The Coca-Cola Kid*   d) Matt Dillon

20. a) Whose life was portrayed in the movie *Lady Sings the Blues*, and b) who played the leading role?

21. Who played the a) John Garfield and b) Lana Turner roles in the 1981 remake of *The Postman Always Rings Twice*?

22. Fred Astaire and Ginger Rogers's only film in color was also their last together. Name it.

23. What real-life sports figures were portrayed in these films?
    a) *The Pride of the Yankees*
    b) *Raging Bull*
    c) *Fear Strikes Out*
    d) *The Pride of St. Louis*

24. a) What movie gave us Travis Bickle, and b) who played him?

25. Who played the ''misters'' in these movies?
    a) *Mr. Hulot's Holiday*
    b) *Mr. Mom*
    c) *Mr. Smith Goes to Washington*
    d) *Mr. Deeds Goes to Town*

Score_____

HOORAY FOR HOLLYWOOD: ANSWERS

1. a) *Sid and Nancy*, b) *Melvyn and Howard*, c) *Harold and Maude*, d) *Harry and Tonto*.
2. a) Albert Finney, b) Peter Ustinov.
3. c) *Li'l Abner*.

4. Ruth Warrick.

5. a) *Vertigo*, b) *Suspicion*, c) *The Man Who Knew Too Much*, d) *Lifeboat*.

6. George A. Romero.

7. a) Robert Schumann, b) Frederic Chopin, c) Franz Liszt.

8. a) *On Golden Pond*, b) Henry Fonda, c) Jane Fonda.

9. a) *The Lion in Winter*, b) Barbra Streisand.

10. James Earl Jones.

11. b) *The Spy Who Loved Me*.

12. a) Don Vito Corleone, b) *The Godfather* and *The Godfather, Part II*.

13. a) alcoholism, b) racism, c) vampirism, d) escapism.

14. Extra-Terrestrial.

15. a) John Irving, b) Peter Benchley, c) Frank Herbert, d) Thomas Mann.

16. a) Loretta Lynn, b) Patsy Cline, c) Hank Williams.

17. a) *The Strange Case of Dr. Jekyll and Mr. Hyde*, b) Robert Louis Stevenson.

18. a) bicycle racing, b) beauty contests, c) piano competitions, d) high school basketball.

19. a) Matt Dillon, b) Charles Grodin, c) Ralph Macchio, d) Eric Roberts.

20. a) Billie Holiday, b) Diana Ross.

21. a) Jack Nicholson, b) Jessica Lange.

22. *The Barkleys of Broadway*.

23. a) Lou Gehrig, b) Jake LaMotta, c) Jimmy Piersall, d) Dizzy Dean.

24. a) *Taxi Driver*, b) Robert De Niro.

25. a) Jacques Tati, b) Michael Keaton, c) James Stewart, d) Gary Cooper.

Common Knowledge
3

1. Who said, on passing through New York customs, "I have nothing to declare except my genius"?

2. A sixth official language (in addition to English, Chinese, French, Spanish, and Russian) was recognized by the United Nations General Assembly in 1973. What was it?

3. Place these planets in proper order from closest to the Sun to farthest:
    a) Mars
    b) Saturn
    c) Uranus
    d) Jupiter

4. Where would one find stamens and pistils?

5. His first single record was "That's All Right," with "Blue Moon of Kentucky" on the flipside. Who was he?

6. Author Mary Ann Evans is better known under what name?

7. What do these scientists study?
   a) icthyologist
   b) lepidopterist
   c) ornithologist
   d) selenologist

8. a) What was known as "Seward's Folly," and b) why?

9. This Nobel Prize–winner heads a labor union in Poland. Name a) the man and b) the union.

10. In what states are these well-known racetracks located?
    a) Churchill Downs
    b) Hialeah
    c) Belmont
    d) Pimlico

11. Ruth St. Denis and Ted Shawn were pioneers in this art form. Name it.

12. Turkey, the USSR, Romania, and Bulgaria all border this body of water. What is it?

13. Her suitor abandons her when her father threatens disinheritance, and she in turn rejects the suitor when he returns after her father's death. Name—
    a) the novel that tells the story
    b) its author
    c) the title of the play and movie adapted from the novel

14. He fought and won the last bare-knuckles championship bout. Who was this boxer?

15. IBM introduced it in 1965. What is it?

16. Which of these words does *not* belong with the others, and why?
    a) diffident
    b) loquacious
    c) voluble
    d) garrulous

17. He took his stand in 1521 at the Diet of Worms. Who was he?

18. A hit play by Neil Simon inspired this hit TV series starring Jack Klugman and Tony Randall. Name a) the play/series, and the characters played by b) Klugman and c) Randall.

19. Our Sun is located in this galaxy. What is it called?

20. Complete the names of these pop/rock groups:
    a) Bob Marley and the —
    b) Sly and the —
    c) Big Brother and the —
    d) Buddy Holly and the —

21. What were Neil Armstrong's words on first setting foot on the moon?

22. In what wars did these forts play a role?
    a) Ft. Sumter
    b) Ft. Duquesne
    c) Ft. McHenry
    d) Ft. Ticonderoga

23. a) What musical works are collectively known as the Savoy Operas, and b) why are they so called?

23. A 1938 radio adaptation of this novel convinced many listeners that the earth was being invaded by Mars. Name—
   a) the novel
   b) its author
   c) its radio adapter

24. In what country is Timbuktu, as in the expression "from here to Timbuktu"?

Score_____

COMMON KNOWLEDGE 3:
ANSWERS

1. Oscar Wilde.
2. Arabic.
3. a) Mars, b) Jupiter, c) Saturn, d) Uranus.
4. In flowers.
5. Elvis Presley.
6. George Eliot.
7. a) fish, b) butterflies and moths, c) birds, d) the moon.
8. a) Alaska b) was purchased from Russia by Secretary of State William H. Seward in 1867, an investment many considered foolish at the time.
9. a) Lech Walesa heads b) Solidarity.
10. a) Kentucky, b) Florida, c) New York, d) Maryland.
11. Modern dance.
12. The Black Sea.
13. a) *Washington Square*, b) Henry James, c) *The Heiress*.
14. John L. Sullivan.
15. The word processor.
16. A *diffident* person is shy and withdrawn; the other words all mean outgoing, talkative.
17. Martin Luther.

18. a) *The Odd Couple*, b) Oscar Madison, c) Felix Unger.
19. The Milky Way.
20. a) Wailers, b) Family Stone, c) Holding Company, d) Crickets.
21. "That's one small step for [a] man, one giant leap for mankind."
22. a) Civil War, b) French and Indian Wars, c) War of 1812, d) American Revolution.
23. a) The operas of Gilbert and Sullivan were first performed at b) the Savoy Theatre, London.
24. a) *The War of the Worlds*, b) H. G. Wells, c) Orson Welles.
25. The Republic of Mali in West Africa.

Le Mot Juste

Substitute the appropriate foreign word or phrase for the English words in **boldface** in the following sentences:

1. Beethoven's Ninth Symphony is considered by many to be his **greatest work**.

2. The critics praised Horowitz's brilliant piano performance as a **demonstration of the highest technical skill**.

3. Either the chicken came before the egg or **the other way around**.

4. It was often said that President Kennedy had **great and inspiring leadership quality**.

5. **"Have a good trip,"** she cried as the ship pulled away from the pier.

6. I don't like change; let's maintain the **way things are**.

7. I can't put my finger on it, the man just had a certain **indefinable quality about him**.

8. His experience on an **Israeli collective farm** taught him responsibility.

9. Though she never trained professionally, she is an **enthusiastic devotee** of ballet.

10. Let's go to Las Vegas and live **the good life** for the weekend.

11. The cook was given **complete freedom** to prepare the meal as he saw fit.

12. "You've got a lot of **cheeky aggressiveness**," she said when the salesman called for the third time.

13. Rather than surrender, the Japanese officer committed **ritual suicide**.

14. Entering the sacred shrine was strictly **forbidden** to foreigners by the natives.

15. Michaelangelo's **depiction of the Virgin Mary mourning over the dead body of Jesus** is among the most moving works on this theme.

16. Our trip to Paris was only **so-so**.

17. Lotte Lehman was renowned for her singing of **German art songs**.

18. **Time flies** when you're having fun.

19. His **restless urge to travel** drove him to the four corners of the world.

20. Let's have a little **private talk**, just you and I.

21. The artist's skill at **effects of optical illusion** made you believe you could step right into his painting.

22. "And that," said the attorney to the jurors, "is our case **in its entirety**."

23. Let's try to bridge our communication gap through **a common hybrid language**.

24. I don't know how this venture will turn out, but **whatever will be, will be**.

25. We'll have to have a yard sale to get rid of all these **assorted little knick-knacks**.

Score_____

LE MOT JUSTE: ANSWERS

1. *meisterwerk.*
2. *tour de force.*
3. *vice versa.*
4. *charisma.*
5. *bon voyage.*
6. *status quo.*
7. *je ne sais quoi.*
8. *kibbutz.*
9. *aficionado.*
10. *la dolce vita.*
11. *carte blanche.*
12. *chutzpah.*
13. *hara kiri.*
14. *taboo.*
15. *pietà.*
16. *comme çi, comme ça.*

17. *lieder.*
18. *tempus fugit.*
19. **wanderlust.**
20. *tête-à-tête.*
21. *trompe l'oeil.*
22. *in toto.*
23. *lingua franca.*
24. *que será será.*
25. *tchotchkes.*

Accentuate the Negative

Which person/place/thing does *not* belong in the following groups? Explain why.

1. a) Oscar Wilde
   b) George Bernard Shaw
   c) Sean O'Casey
   d) Samuel Beckett
   e) Eugene O'Neill

2. a) *Gigi*
   b) *Yankee Doodle Dandy*
   c) *An American in Paris*
   d) *Meet Me in St. Louis*
   e) *The Band Wagon*

3. a) Venus
   b) Jupiter
   c) Uranus
   d) The Moon
   e) Earth

4. a) The Pyramids of Egypt
   b) The Hanging Gardens of Babylon

   c) The Parthenon
   d) The Lighthouse of Alexandria
   e) The Colossus at Rhodes

5. a) Ghana
   b) Guinea
   c) Grenada
   d) Guyana
   e) Guatemala

6. a) Baton Rouge
   b) Concord
   c) Dubuque
   d) Harrisburg
   e) Columbia

7. a) Lyndon B. Johnson
   b) Richard Nixon
   c) Harry S Truman
   d) Jimmy Carter
   e) Gerald Ford

8. a) bronze
   b) zinc
   c) iron
   d) copper
   e) lead

9. a) George Washington
   b) Benjamin Franklin
   c) John Hancock
   d) Thomas Jefferson
   e) John Adams

10. a) *La Traviata*
   b) *La Boheme*

c) *Aida*
d) *Il Trovatore*
e) *Rigoletto*

11. a) Chicago Cubs
    b) Montreal Expos
    c) Philadelphia Phillies
    d) Atlanta Braves
    e) St. Louis Cardinals

12. a) Chronicles
    b) Numbers
    c) Hebrews
    d) Psalms
    e) Proverbs

13. a) Amherst
    b) Harvard
    c) Yale
    d) Brown
    e) Columbia

14. a) Richard Burton
    b) Eddie Fisher
    c) John Warner
    d) Mike Todd
    e) Montgomery Clift

15. a) PBS
    b) ABC
    c) CBS
    d) HBO
    e) NBC

16. a) Christopher Columbus
    b) Vasco da Gama

c) Amerigo Vespucci
  d) Giovanni da Verrazano
  e) Juan Ponce de Leon

17. a) John Steinbeck
  b) Ernest Hemingway
  c) Sinclair Lewis
  d) William Faulkner
  e) F. Scott Fitzgerald

18. a) pluralism
  b) surrealism
  c) cubism
  d) constructivism
  e) futurism

19. a) lion
  b) giraffe
  c) tiger
  d) rhinoceros
  e) elephant

20. a) *The War of the Worlds*
  b) *Around the World in Eighty Days*
  c) *The Time Machine*
  d) *The First Men in the Moon*
  e) *The Invisible Man*

21. a) The Wars of the Roses
  b) The Seven Years' War
  c) The Thirty Years' War
  d) King Philip's War
  e) The Franco-Prussian War

22. a) *The Music Man*
  b) *South Pacific*

c) *Pal Joey*
d) *The Sound of Music*
e) *Oklahoma*

23. a) Bob Dylan
    b) James Taylor
    c) Paul Simon
    d) Bruce Springsteen
    e) Billy Joel

24. a) quark
    b) quasar
    c) neutron
    d) meson
    e) electron

25. a) 1
    b) 10
    c) 100
    d) 10,000
    e) 1,000,000

Score_____

ACCENTUATE THE NEGATIVE: ANSWERS

1. Eugene O'Neill was an American playwright, the others were Irish.
2. *Yankee Doodle Dandy* is the only black-and-white film among these technicolor movie musicals.
3. The Moon is a satellite that orbits the Earth; the others are planets that orbit the sun.
4. The Parthenon is the only one of these ancient structures that is not one of the Seven Wonders of the World.

5. Grenada is the only island nation among these countries.

6. All are state capitals except Dubuque.

7. All these U.S. presidents except Jimmy Carter served first as vice-president.

8. Bronze is a metallic alloy of copper and tin; the others are pure elements.

9. George Washington is the only one of this group who did not sign the Declaration of Independence.

10. *La Boheme* was written by Puccini, the other operas by Verdi.

11. The Atlanta Braves are in the National League West division, the others in the East division.

12. Hebrews is a book of the New Testament, the others of the Old.

13. Amherst is the only college here not in the Ivy League.

14. All married Elizabeth Taylor except Montgomery Clift.

15. HBO is the only cable station among these networks.

16. Vasco da Gama was the only one of these European explorers not to have visited the New World.

17. Alone among these American authors, F. Scott Fitzgerald did not receive the Nobel Prize for Literature.

18. Pluralism is not an art movement; the others are.

19. These animals are all native to Africa except the tiger.

20. *Around the World in Eighty Days* was written by Jules Verne, the other books by H. G. Wells.

21. King Philip's War was fought in the New World, the others in Europe.

22. Richard Rodgers wrote the music for all these shows except *The Music Man*.

23. Billy Joel is a piano man; the others primarily play guitar.

24. These are all subatomic particles with the exception of a quasar, which is a distant starlike object.

25. Unlike the other numbers, the number 10 does not have an even square root.

A Sporting Chance

1. This baseball player broke Babe Ruth's single-season home run record. Name:
   a) the player
   b) the number of home runs he hit
   c) the year he did it
   d) the team he played on

2. Awarded annually by the Downtown Athletic Club of New York, it goes to an outstanding college athlete. a) What is it called, and b) in what sport is it awarded?

3. Known as the Great One, he has scored more goals than any other player in National Hockey League history. Who is he?

4. This former Wimbledon and U.S. open tennis champion beat one great woman player and lost to another in celebrated exhibition matches. Name a) the man, and b) c) the two women.

5. Which of these golfers never won the Professional Golfers Association (PGA) tournament?

a) Arnold Palmer
b) Jack Nicklaus
c) Ben Hogan
d) Lee Trevino

6. An Olympic gold medalist in track and field, she later won ten major golf titles. Name this great athlete.

7. Baseball managers Walter Alston, Connie Mack, and Casey Stengel share this rare distinction. What is it?

8. Sometimes called the Kentucky Derby for trotters, this prestigious harness race is known as what?

9. In what sports are these trophies awarded?
    a) The Stanley Cup
    b) The America's Cup
    c) The Federation Cup
    d) The Ryder Cup

10. One of these horses did *not* win the Triple Crown. Which one?
    a) Whirlaway
    b) Man O'War
    c) Citation
    d) Secretariat

11. These two brothers are both multiple winners of the Indianapolis 500 auto race. Who are they?

12. He is the only player in National Basketball Association history to score 100 points in a single game. Name—
    a) the player
    b) the team he played on in this game
    c) the team he played against in this game

13. Sandy Koufax, Tom Seaver, and Jim Palmer all won this three times. a) What is it, and b) who won it *four* times?

14. Name the woman runner who won the New York City Marathon nine times from 1978 to 1988.

15. This former New York Knicks basketball star became a United States senator. Who is he?

16. Bjorn Borg is the only man to have done this in five consecutive years. What was it?

17. The first black player and the first black manager in the major leagues happened to share the same surname. Identify a) b) the two men, and c) d) the teams on which the one first played and the other first managed.

18. Match these stadiums with the baseball teams that play in them:

a) Shea Stadium	a) Toronto Blue Jays
b) The SkyDome	b) Baltimore Orioles
c) Veterans Stadium	c) New York Mets
d) Memorial Stadium	d) Philadelphia Phillies

19. What is the Vince Lombardi Trophy awarded for?

20. National Football League statistics place Fran Tarkenton first, Johnny Unitas second, and Sonny Jurgensen third. First, second, and third in what?

21. These twin brothers finished first and second in the 1984 Olympic slalom event. Name them.

22. Edson Arantes do Nascimento is better known a) under what name and b) in what sport?

22. Who was the first man to run the mile in less than four minutes?

23. He pitched the only perfect game in World Series history. Name—
   a) the player
   b) the team he played on
   c) the team he beat
   d) the year he did it

24. Who was the first woman to swim the English Channel?

Score_____

A SPORTING CHANCE: ANSWERS

1. a) Roger Maris, b) 61, c) 1961, d) the New York Yankees.
2. a) The Heisman Trophy, b) football.
3. Wayne Gretzky.
4. a) Bobby Riggs, b) Margaret Smith Court, c) Billie Jean King.
5. a) Arnold Palmer.
6. Babe Didrikson Zaharias.
7. They are all members of the Baseball Hall of Fame.
8. The Hambletonian.
9. a) hockey, b) yacht racing, c) tennis, d) golf.
10. b) Man O'War.
11. Al Unser, Sr. and Bobby Unser.
12. a) Wilt Chamberlain, b) Philadelphia Warriors, c) New York Knicks.
13. a) The Cy Young Award, b) Steve Carlton.
14. Grete Waitz.
15. Senator Bill Bradley of New Jersey.
16. Winning the Wimbledon singles tennis title.

17. a) Jackie Robinson, player, b) Frank Robinson, manager, c) Brooklyn Dodgers (Jackie), d) Cleveland Indians (Frank).
18. a) New York Mets, b) Toronto Blue Jays, c) Philadelphia Phillies, d) Baltimore Orioles.
19. Winning football's Super Bowl.
20. Completed touchdown passes.
21. Phil and Steve Mahre.
22. a) Pelé, b) soccer.
23. Roger Bannister.
24. a) Don Larson, b) New York Yankees, c) Brooklyn Dodgers, d) 1956.
25. Gertrude Ederle.

Common Knowledge
4

1. What historical figures are associated with these ships?
   a) *Half Moon*
   b) *Golden Hind*
   c) *Bon Homme Richard*
   d) *Beagle*

2. TV's Six Million Dollar Man had a female counterpart. What was she called?

3. What nuclear physicist is sometimes called the Father of the Hydrogen Bomb?

4. Which of these words does *not* belong with the others, and why?
   a) soporific
   b) narcotic
   c) ebullient
   d) somnolent

5. This character narrates *Moby Dick* by Herman Melville. What is his name?

6. Richard D'Oyle Carte first produced these celebrated musical works. What are they?

7. This last czar of Russia was killed by the Bolsheviks in 1918. Who was he?

8. Connect these Greek gods with their special domains:
   a) Ares   a) wind
   b) Eros   b) dawn
   c) Eos   c) love
   d) Aeolus   d) war

9. The first of these historical novels by Sir Walter Scott gives the whole series its name. What is it?

10. a) Who led whom on the Long March, and b) why?

11. Indiana, Kentucky, Tennessee, and one other state fall into both the Eastern and Central time zones. What is the fourth state?

12. Photosynthesis takes place—
   a) in a test tube?
   b) in a leaf?
   c) in a rainbow?
   d) in a flower?

13. What is the difference between a biannual and a biennial event?

14. *"Et tu, Brute?"* a) Who speaks the line b) to whom c) in what play d) by what author?

15. Who was known as Good Queen Bess?

16. In United States history, who was the first woman—
   a) to serve as a member of the cabinet?
   b) to run for vice-president?
   c) to be appointed to the Supreme Court?

17. American poets Amy, James Russell, and Robert share a common surname. What is it?

18. This revolutionary leader gave his name to a South American country. Name a) him and b) the country.

19. What is a monotheist?

20. He won Nobel Prizes in both peace and chemistry. Name him.

21. Identify these items from a French menu:
    a) *escargots*
    b) *moules*
    c) *champignons*
    d) *pommes de terre*

22. Lewis W. Hine, Paul Strand, and Eugene Atget are known for what?

23. Select the correct word in the following sentences:
    a) Through this example, he was able to (affect, effect) change.
    b) He took his exercise on a (stationary, stationery) bicycle.
    c) Persecution drove him to (emigrate, immigrate) from his homeland.
    d) The doctor told him to (lay, lie) down on the examining table.

24. What is the fastest land animal?

25. *The Diary of a Young Girl* is better known by its stage and movie title. What is it?

Score_____

COMMON KNOWLEDGE 4: ANSWERS

1. a) Henry Hudson, b) Sir Francis Drake, c) John Paul Jones, d) Charles Darwin.
2. The Bionic Woman.
3. Edward Teller.
4. *Ebullient* means energized, lively; the others all suggest sleepiness.
5. Ishmael.
6. The Gilbert and Sullivan operas.
7. Nicholas II.
8. a) war, b) love, c) dawn, d) wind.
9. *Waverly.*
10. a) Mao Zedong led the Chinese Communists b) in this escape from the government forces of Chiang Kai-shek.
11. Florida.
12. In a leaf.
13. The biannual takes place twice a year, the biennial every two years.
14. a) Julius Caesar, b) Brutus, c) *Julius Caesar,* d) William Shakespeare.
15. Queen Elizabeth I of England.
16. a) Frances Perkins (Secretary of Labor, 1933), b) Geraldine Ferraro (1984), c) Sandra Day O'Connor (1981).
17. Lowell.
18. a) Simon Bolivar, b) Bolivia.
19. A person who believes in one god.
20. Linus Pauling.
21. a) snails, b) mussels, c) mushrooms, d) potatoes.
22. Their photography.
23. a) effect, b) stationary, c) emigrate, d) lie.
24. The cheetah.
25. *The Diary of Anne Frank.*

The Name's the Same

Each member of the following threesomes shares a common surname with the others. Identify all of them by their full names.

1. a) a civil rights leader
   b) a president of the United States
   c) a "bad" pop singer

2. a) half a comedy team
   b) a Victorian novelist
   c) a character played by Mickey Rooney

3. a) a rebel leader
   b) a country singer/actor
   c) a jazz innovator

4. a) a playwright
   b) a country singer/songwriter
   c) a comedian/actor

5. a) a cinematic beauty
   b) an army chief of staff
   c) a singer/songwriter

6. a) a comedian/actor
    b) a novelist
    c) an explorer

7. a) a novelist
    b) a country singer
    c) a jazz composer/arranger

8. a) a novelist
    b) a movie queen
    c) a fictional belle

9. a) an English actor
    b) his actress daughter
    c) his other actress daughter

10. a) TV's Baretta
     b) TV's Miss Kitty
     c) a poet

11. a) a cosmetics queen
     b) a pianist
     c) his actor son

12. a) a TV host
     b) a World War II general
     c) a country singer

13. a) a rock singer
     b) an entrepreneur
     c) a movie star

14. a) an architect
     b) a composer
     c) a TV host

15. a) a legendary magazine editor
    b) a pop singer
    c) an actress

16. a) a civil rights leader
    b) a bestselling writer
    c) a singer/songwriter

17. a) a movie actor
    b) his actress daughter
    c) his actor son

18. a) a playwright
    b) a bandleader
    c) a dancer/actress

19. a) a movie idol
    b) a singer/songwriter
    c) a TV newsman/host

20. a) a country singer
    b) a humorist
    c) a movie cowboy

21. a) a sportswriter
    b) an economist
    c) an actress

22. a) a comic actor/writer/director
    b) a patriot
    c) a sports announcer

23. a) an operatic soprano
    b) a novelist
    c) a ballerina

24. a) an auto maker
    b) a country singer
    c) a movie director

25. a) a newspaper publisher
    b) a choreographer
    c) an evangelist

Score_____

THE NAME'S THE SAME: ANSWERS

1. a) Jesse Jackson, b) Andrew Jackson, c) Michael Jackson.
2. a) Oliver Hardy, b) Thomas Hardy, c) Andy Hardy.
3. a) Jefferson Davis, b) Mac Davis, c) Miles Davis.
4. a) Tennessee Williams, b) Hank Williams, c) Robin Williams.
5. a) Elizabeth Taylor, b) Maxwell Taylor, c) James Taylor.
6. a) Jerry (or Richard) Lewis, b) Sinclair Lewis, c) Meriwether Lewis.
7. a) James Jones, b) George Jones, c) Quincy Jones.
8. a) John O'Hara, b) Maureen O'Hara, c) Scarlett O'Hara.
9. a) Michael Redgrave, b) Vanessa Redgrave, c) Lynn Redgrave.
10. a) Robert Blake, b) Amanda Blake, c) William Blake.
11. a) Helena Rubinstein, b) Arthur Rubinstein, c) John Rubinstein.
12. a) Dick Clark, b) Mark Clark, c) Roy Clark.
13. a) Tina Turner, b) Ted Turner, c) Kathleen Turner.
14. a) Louis Sullivan, b) Sir Arthur Sullivan, c) Ed Sullivan.
15. a) Harold Ross, b) Diana Ross, c) Katharine Ross.
16. a) Martin Luther King, Jr., b) Stephen King, c) Carole King.
17. a) Henry Fonda, b) Jane Fonda, c) Peter Fonda.
18. a) Arthur Miller, b) Glenn Miller, c) Ann Miller.

19. a) Paul Newman, b) Randy Newman, c) Edwin Newman.
20. a) Kenny Rogers, b) Will Rogers, c) Roy Rogers.
21. a) Red Smith, b) Adam Smith, c) Maggie Smith.
22. a) Woody Allen, b) Ethan Allen, c) Mel Allen.
23. a) Eileen Farrell, b) James T. Farrell, c) Suzanne Farrell.
24. a) Henry Ford, b) Tennessee Ernie Ford, c) John Ford.
25. a) Katharine Graham, b) Martha Graham, c) Billy Graham.

Of Cabbages and Kings

1. Who wrote the following novels?
   a) *King Solomon's Mines*
   b) *All the King's Men*
   c) *The King Must Die*
   d) *Captains and the Kings*

2. What is known as the sport of kings?

3. John Hancock made his signature on the Declaration of Independence large enough to enable what king to read it?

4. Who "looked down on the feast of Stephen"?

5. This female king ruled over courts throughout the world. Who is she?

6. a) What is the source of the famous movie line, "Where's the rest of me?" and b) what actor spoke it?

7. a) What British king gave up his crown for the woman he loved, and b) what was her name?

8. Who wrote, "In the country of the blind, the one-eyed man is king"?

9. The "King of Thule" aria is sung—
    a) by what character?
    b) in what opera?
    c) by what composer?

10. This hirsute king is a true kingmaker in the ring. Who is he?

11. Where is the King Ranch?

12. Those who opened this Egyptian King's tomb were said to have been cursed. What was his name?

13. Kingston is the capital of what Caribbean nation?

14. What did Old King Cole call for?

15. From what Shakespeare plays do the following lines come?
    a) "A horse! a horse! my kingdom for a horse!"
    b) "For God's sake, let us sit upon the ground
       And tell sad stories of the death of kings"
    c) "The play's the thing
       Wherein I'll catch the conscience of the King"
    d) "Uneasy lies the head that wears a crown"

16. Who was the King of Troy at the time of the Trojan War?

17. What are kinglets and kingfishers?

18. (Who) of the following was *not* a wife of King Henry VIII?

a) Katharine of Aragon
b) Catherine Howard
c) Catherine de' Medici
d) Catherine Parr

19. Only during this special move may the king on a chessboard move more than one space. What is it called?

20. a) Provide the first line of this rhyming couplet: "I'm sure we should all be as happy as kings," and b) identify its author.

21. Fill in the blanks:
King Arthur's wife a) _____ was unfaithful to him with b) _____, whose son c) _____ went on a quest for d) _____.

22. In the expression "from here to kingdom come," where *is* kingdom come?

23. The so-called Authorized Version of the Bible is also known as what?

24. Kings County, New York, is better known by what name?

25. This king and his queen were both guillotined during the French Revolution. Who are they?

Score_____

OF CABBAGES AND KINGS: ANSWERS

1. a) H. Rider Haggard, b) Robert Penn Warren, c) Mary Renault, d) Taylor Caldwell.

2. Horse racing.

3. George III of England.

4. Good King Wenceslaus.

5. Billie Jean King, tennis star.

6. a) *King's Row*, b) Ronald Reagan.

7. a) Edward VIII, b) Wallis Warfield Simpson.

8. H. G. Wells.

9. a) Marguerite, b) *Faust*, c) Charles Gounod.

10. Don King, boxing promoter.

11. In Texas.

12. King Tutankhamen.

13. Jamaica.

14. His pipe, his bowl, and his fiddlers three.

15. a) *Richard III*, b) *Richard II*, c) *Hamlet*, d) *Henry IV, Part 2*.

16. Priam.

17. Birds.

18. c) Catherine de' Medici.

19. Castling.

20. a) "The world is so full of a number of things," b) Robert Louis Stevenson.

21. a) Guinevere, b) Launcelot, c) Galahad, d) the Holy Grail.

22. The next world, or life after death.

23. The King James Version.

24. Brooklyn.

25. Louis XVI and Marie Antoinette.

Family Affairs

1. What were the names of the *Little Women* in Louisa May Alcott's novel?

2. Who wrote the following novels?
   - a) *Fathers and Sons*
   - b) *Sons and Lovers*
   - c) *Dombey and Son*
   - d) *Native Son*

3. Yul Brynner, among others, starred in the film version of this Russian classic. Name a) the title of this fraternal novel and b) its author.

4. Name the three Gabor sisters and their mother.

5. The song "Brother Can You Spare a Dime?" was popular during what period of American history?

6. a) What is the source of the line, "And we are his sisters and his cousins and his aunts," and b) who is *he*?

7. In the film *Father of the Bride*, who played a) the father, b) the bride, and c) the mother of the bride?

8. What is the meaning, in politics, of the term *favorite son*?

9. Who composed these operas?
   a) *The Daughter of the Regiment*
   b) *The Mother of Us All*
   c) *Suor (Sister) Angelica*
   d) *The Bartered Bride*

10. What is the proverbial "mother of invention"?

11. Name the actor/fathers of these actor/sons:
   a) Jeff and Beau
   b) David and Keith
   c) Emilio and Charlie

12. The play *My Sister Eileen* became a Broadway musical. Name a) the show and b) its composer.

13. What are the relationships between these same-name presidents of the United States?
   a) John Adams and John Quincy Adams
   b) William Henry Harrison and Benjamin Harrison
   c) Theodore Roosevelt and Franklin Delano Roosevelt

14. Who wrote these plays?
   a) *Uncle Vanya*
   b) *Mother Courage*
   c) *All My Sons*
   d) *The Children's Hour*

15. a) What actress played Princess Leia in *Star Wars*, and b) who are her famous parents?

16. What is known as the City of Brotherly Love?

17. Who wrote *Le Père Goriot* and *La Cousine Bette*?

18. The father is known as the Elder, the son as the Younger. Name these famous same-name German artists.

19. Bret Harte's stories helped to make famous this gold-bearing area of California. What is its familial and familiar name?

20. a) Who is the father that speaks the line, "This is my son, mine own Telemachus," and b) what is its source?

21. In Shakespeare, this character's mother marries his father's brother. Name a) the character, b) his mother, c) his father, and d) his uncle.

22. A boy's physical attraction toward his mother and hostility toward his father is known as what in Freudian psychology?

23. What does D.A.R. stand for?

24. Match these films with their stars:
    - a) *Auntie Mame*
    - b) *Mother Wore Tights*
    - c) *Father Goose*
    - d) *Cousins*

    - a) Rosalind Russell
    - b) Leslie Caron
    - c) Betty Grable
    - d) Isabella Rossellini

25. This organization of patriots boasted Samuel Adams and Paul Revere among its members. Name it.

Score_____

FAMILY AFFAIRS: ANSWERS

1. Jo, Amy, Meg, and Beth.
2. a) Ivan Turgenev, b) D. H. Lawrence, c) Charles Dickens, d) Richard Wright.
3. a) *The Brothers Karamazov*, b) Feodor Dostoevsky.
4. Zsa Zsa, Eva, Magda, and Jolie
5. The Great Depression.
6. a) *H.M.S. Pinafore* by Gilbert and Sullivan, b) Sir Joseph Porter.
7. a) Spencer Tracy, b) Elizabeth Taylor, c) Joan Bennett.
8. Someone who receives an honorary nomination for the presidency by his own state delegation.
9. a) Gaetano Donizetti, b) Virgil Thomson, c) Giacomo Puccini, d) Bedřich Smetana.
10. Necessity.
11. a) Lloyd Bridges, b) John Carradine, c) Martin Sheen.
12. a) *Wonderful Town*, b) Leonard Bernstein.
13. a) John Adams was father of John Quincy; b) William Henry Harrison was grandfather of Benjamin; c) Theodore and Franklin Delano Roosevelt were distant cousins.
14. a) Anton Chekhov, b) Berthold Brecht, c) Arthur Miller, d) Lillian Hellman.
15. a) Carrie Fisher, b) Eddie Fisher and Debbie Reynolds.
16. Philadelphia, Pennsylvania.
17. Honoré de Balzac.
18. Hans Holbein.
19. The Mother Lode.
20. a) Ulysses, b) the poem "Ulysses" by Alfred, Lord Tennyson.
21. a) Hamlet, b) Gertrude, c) Hamlet, d) Claudius.
22. Oedipus complex.
23. Daughters of the American Revolution.
24. a) Rosalind Russell, b) Betty Grable, c) Leslie Caron, d) Isabella Rossellini.
25. Sons of Liberty.

Common Knowledge
5

1. The characters John Steed and Emma Peel appeared in this TV series. Name a) the series, and the actors who played b) Steed and c) Peel.

2. Where are these world-class art museums located?
    a) The Metropolitan
    b) The Louvre
    c) The Prado
    d) The Hermitage

3. Whose statue dominates London's Trafalgar Square?

4. One sister tended to Jesus's needs, the other to household chores. a) Who were they, and b) which one had "chosen well," according to Jesus?

5. This essay by Thoreau influenced such later passive-resisters as Gandhi and Martin Luther King, Jr. Name the essay.

6. How long are the following units of time?
    a) fortnight

b) olympiad
c) decade
d) millennium

7. Specify the freezing and boiling points a) on the Fahrenheit scale and b) on the Celcius scale.

8. When the protagonist's former lover kills her husband's lover in a car accident, the victim's husband shoots and kills the protagonist because it was his car. Name a) the novel that tells this story and b) its author.

9. What do dodos, moas, and great auks have in common?

10. It took place on board the USS *Missouri* in 1945. What happened?

11. From a critical point of view, what is wrong with the following sentence?
> Despite trials and tribulations too numerous to mention, he remained, in the long run, as cool as a cucumber.

12. Which of these words does *not* belong with the others, and why?
   a) translucent
   b) limpid
   c) nebulous
   d) pellucid

13. Who was the first black to be appointed a Supreme Court justice?

14. What is sometimes called the October Revolution?

15. Name the doctor who performed the world's first human heart transplant.

16. What groups are these rock-and-rollers most closely associated with?
   - a) Jim Morrison
   - b) Sting
   - c) Mike Love
   - d) Grace Slick

17. What countries opposed each other in the Falkland Islands war of 1982?

18. Define the following terms:
   - a) homonym
   - b) synonym
   - c) eponym

19. Novelist Evan Hunter writes mysteries under this equally well-known pen name. What is it?

20. Name the wars in which these events took place:
   - a) Charge of the Light Brigade
   - b) Tet Offensive
   - c) Inchon Invasion
   - d) Gallipoli Campaign

21. His expedition was the first to circumnavigate the globe, but he was killed along the way. Who was this explorer?

22. Who wrote the poem *Howl*?

23. Connect these choreographers with their dances:
   - a) Jerome Robbins
   - b) George Balanchine
   - c) Martha Graham
   - d) Agnes De Mille

   - a) *Dances at a Gathering*
   - b) *Appalachian Spring*
   - c) *Rodeo*
   - d) *Jewels*

24. a) Who in history "crossed the Rubicon," and b) what does the expression mean today?

25. Name the fictional works and their authors in which these residences are found:
    a) Manderley
    b) Tara
    c) 44 Baker Street
    d) Toad Hall

Score_____

COMMON KNOWLEDGE 5: ANSWERS

1. a) *The Avengers*, b) Patrick Macnee, c) Diana Rigg.
2. a) New York City, b) Paris, c) Madrid, d) Leningrad.
3. Admiral Horatio Nelson's.
4. a) Mary and Martha, b) Mary.
5. "Civil Disobedience"
6. a) two weeks, b) four years, c) ten years, d) 1,000 years.
7. a) 32° and 212° Fahrenheit, b) 0° and 100° Celcius.
8. a) *The Great Gatsby*, b) F. Scott Fitzgerald.
9. They are all extinct birds.
10. Japan formally surrendered to the United States, ending World War II.
11. It is cliché-ridden: *trials and tribulations, too numerous to mention, in the long run,* and *cool as a cucumber* are all clichés.
12. *Nebulous* means vague; the others suggest degrees of clarity.
13. Thurgood Marshall.
14. The Bolshevik or Russian Revolution of 1917.
15. Christian N. Barnard.

16. a) The Doors, b) The Police, c) The Beach Boys, d) The Jefferson Airplane (or Starship).

17. Great Britain (England) and Argentina.

18. a) A word that sounds like another but has a different meaning; b) a word that is different in sound from another but has the same or similar meaning; c) the name of a person from whom the name of a place or thing is derived.

19. Ed McBain.

20. a) Crimean War, b) Vietnam War, c) Korean War, d) World War I.

21. Ferdinand Magellan.

22. Allen Ginsberg.

23. a) *Dances at a Gathering*, b) *Jewels*, c) *Appalachian Spring*, d) *Rodeo*.

24. a) Julius Caesar. b) To cross the Rubicon means to go beyond the point of no return.

25. a) *Rebecca* by Daphne Du Maurier, b) *Gone With the Wind* by Margaret Mitchell, c) the Sherlock Holmes stories by Arthur Conan Doyle, d) *The Wind in the Willows* by Kenneth Grahame.

Famous Firsts

1. Who was called "first in war, first in peace, and first in the hearts of his countrymen"?

2. a) What is the first book of the Old Testament called?
   b) According to that book, what were God's first words?
   c) Who were the first man and woman He created?

3. Who was the first host of NBC's "Tonight Show"?

4. Who wrote the poem "On First Looking Into Chapman's Homer"?

5. Who was the first U.S. president born in the twentieth century?

6. a) Who was the first man to orbit the earth?
   b) Who was the first American in space?
   c) Who was the first American in orbit?

7. *First Blood* introduced what movie superhero?

8. Name a) the first opera performed at the original Metro-

politan Opera House in New York City, and b) the first opera performed at the new Met in Lincoln Center.

9. What is the first deadly sin?

10. Who is usually credited with inventing the first of these devices?
  a) the movable-type printing press
  b) the home sewing machine
  c) the telephone
  d) the wireless telegraph

11. Who discovered the first effective vaccine against polio?

12. The First World War was precipitated by what violent event?

13. Who wrote the novel *First Men in the Moon*?

14. Who was the *real* first man on the moon?

15. Substitute the appropriate "first" phrase for the words in **boldface** below:
  "My a) **initial reaction**," the reporter said, "was that the fire victims suffered only from b) **moderate** burns, and were receiving c) **immediate help** of the d) **highest rank** from paramedics on the scene."

16. A first lieutenant in the army ranks a) just above and b) just below what two officers?

17. The Wright Brothers' first manned flight took place here. Where was it?

18. Who established the First Empire in France?

19. As copilot is to pilot, this person is to a ship's captain. What is he/she called?

20. Provide the first names of these presidents' first ladies:
   a) John Adams
   b) James Madison
   c) Abraham Lincoln
   d) Harry S Truman

21. What European explorers were the first to discover the following:
   a) Pacific Ocean
   b) Mississippi River
   c) Hudson Bay
   d) St. Lawrence River

22. a) Where were the first modern Olympic Games held, and b) in what year?

23. Who was the first man to reach a) the North Pole, and b) the South Pole?

24. Who was a) the first man to fly solo across the Atlantic Ocean, and b) the first woman to do the same?

25. The first major encounter between North and South in the American Civil War is known by two names. a) What are they, and b) which side won?

Score_____

FAMOUS FIRSTS: ANSWERS

1. George Washington.
2. a) Genesis, b) Let there be light, c) Adam and Eve.

3. Steve Allen.

4. John Keats.

5. John F. Kennedy.

6. a) Yuri A. Gagarin, b) Alan B. Shepard, Jr., c) John H. Glenn, Jr.

7. Rambo.

8. a) *Faust* by Charles Gounod, b) *Anthony and Cleopatra* by Samuel Barber.

9. Pride.

10. a) Johan Gutenberg, b) Isaac M. Singer, c) Alexander Graham Bell, d) Guglielmo Marconi.

11. Jonas E. Salk.

12. The assassination of Austrian Archduke Francis Ferdinand at Sarajevo.

13. H. G. Wells.

14. Neil Armstrong.

15. a) first impression, b) first degree, c) first aid, d) first order (or first water).

16. a) above a second lieutenant and b) below a captain.

17. Kitty Hawk, North Carolina.

18. Napoleon Bonaparte.

19. First mate or first officer.

20. a) Abigail, b) Dolly, c) Mary, d) Bess.

21. a) Vasco Nuñez de Balboa, b) Hernando de Soto, c) Henry Hudson, d) Jacques Cartier.

22. a) Athens, Greece, b) 1896.

23. a) Robert E. Peary, b) Roald Amundsen.

24. a) Charles A. Lindbergh, b) Amelia Earhart.

25. a) Bull Run and Manasses, b) the South.

Go for the Gold

1. Sir James Frazer's book *The Golden Bough* deals with—
    a) economics?
    b) anthropology?
    c) botany?
    d) nursery rhymes?

2. What is a "goldbrick" in army slang?

3. What body of water does the Golden Gate Bridge span?

4. Identify these people with "gold" in their surnames:
    a) a Nobel Prize–winning author
    b) a Hollywood mogul
    c) a Supreme Court justice
    d) an anarchist

5. Jason and his crew sought the Golden Fleece in this ship. Name it.

6. Goldie Hawn won a best supporting actress Oscar for her performance in what movie?

7. "Where the Blue of the Night Meets the Gold of the Day" was his theme song. Name the singer.

8. Concerning the novel *The Man With the Golden Arm*—
    a) Who wrote it?
    b) Who played the title role in the movie?
    c) Who directed the movie?

9. What are goldenglow and goldentuft?

10. Gertrude Berg created and played this character for years on radio and television. Name her.

11. Who wrote the novel *The Golden Bowl*?

12. a) In what year did Barry Goldwater run for president of the United States, and b) who defeated him?

13. What mythological king was said to have the golden touch?

14. Match the stars with their "golden" movies:
    a) Sean Connery   a) *Golden Boy*
    b) Eddie Murphy   b) *Goldfinger*
    c) William Holden   c) *The Golden Child*
    d) Charlie Chaplin   d) *The Gold Rush*

15. Name the four actresses who play television's *Golden Girls*.

16. This Italian opera includes characters named Minnie, Jack, and Dick. a) What is its golden English-language title, and b) who composed it?

17. Name a) the poem that concludes with the lines:
    The silver apples of the moon.

The golden apples of the sun.
and b) the poet who wrote it.

18. What is the Golden Rule?

19. Concerning the California Gold Rush—
    a) Who discovered the gold?
    b) Where was it found?
    c) In what year was it found?

20. The art of changing base metals into gold was known as what?

21. Define each of the following with a golden phrase:
    a) They're played on the radio.
    b) Boxers compete in them.
    c) Mark Spitz has seven of them.
    d) They marry for money.

22. Born in Russia and raised in the United States, she achieved her greatest fame in Israel. Who was she?

23. The Three Wise Men brought gifts of gold and what other two substances to the infant Jesus?

24. His "Cross of Gold" speech won him the Democratic nomination for President in 1896. a) Who was he, and b) who beat him in that election?

25. Oliver Goldsmith's only novel concerns a country parson and his family. Name it.

Score_____

GO FOR THE GOLD: ANSWERS

1. b) anthropology.
2. A loafer whose show of working hard is designed to disguise his real inactivity.
3. The Golden Gate, a strait leading from the Pacific Ocean into San Francisco Bay.
4. a) William Golding, b) Samuel Goldwyn, c) Arthur Goldberg, d) Emma Goldman.
5. The *Argo*.
6. *Cactus Flower*.
7. Bing Crosby.
8. a) Nelson Algren, b) Frank Sinatra, c) Otto Preminger.
9. Flowers.
10. Molly Goldberg.
11. Henry James.
12. a) 1964, b) Lyndon B. Johnson.
13. King Midas.
14. a) *Goldfinger*, b) *The Golden Child*, c) *Golden Boy,* d) *The Gold Rush*.
15. a) Bea Arthur, b) Betty White, c) Rue McClanahan, d) Estelle Getty.
16. a) *The Girl of the Golden West*, b) Giacomo Puccini.
17. a) "The Song of the Wandering Aengus," b) William Butler Yeats.
18. The universal moral precept that is usually stated as "Do unto others as you would have others do unto you."
19. a) James W. Marshall, b) near Sutter's Mill, c) 1848.
20. Alchemy.
21. a) golden oldies, b) Golden Gloves, c) Olympic gold medals, d) gold diggers.
22. Golda Meir.
23. Myrrh and frankincense.
24. a) William Jennings Bryan, b) William McKinley.
25. *The Vicar of Wakefield*.

Brush Up Your Shakespeare

1. Generally regarded as Cole Porter's finest Broadway musical, it is based on a Shakespeare play. Name a) the musical and b) the play.

2. Name the Shakespeare plays in which these pairs of lovers appear:
   a) Miranda and Ferdinand
   b) Beatrice and Benedick
   c) Rosalind and Orlando
   d) Viola and Orsino

3. a) What Shakespeare character is described as having "a lean and hungry look"? b) In what play?

4. Name King Lear's three daughters.

5. The character of Sir John Falstaff appears in three Shakespeare plays. Name them.

6. These quotes all come from the same play by Shakespeare. Which one?
   a) "Sweets to the sweet: farewell!"

b) "Now cracks a noble heart"

c) "The lady doth protest too much, methinks"

7. In what Shakespeare play do we find the song, "Who is Sylvia?"

8. What was Shakespeare's hometown?

9. Connect these Shakespeare tragedies with the themes that best fit them:

a) *Hamlet*   a) jealousy
b) *Othello*   b) ambition
c) *Macbeth*   c) pride
d) *Coriolanus*   d) revenge

10. Quote the line that follows each of these from Shakespeare's sonnets:

a) "Shall I compare thee to a summer's day?"
b) "When to the sessions of sweet silent thought"
c) "So long as men can breathe, or eyes can see"
d) "When in disgrace with fortune and men's eyes"

11. In what Shakespeare plays do these real historical battles figure?

a) The Battle of Actium
b) The Battle of Agincourt
c) The Battle of Bosworth Field

12. What was Shakespeare's wife's name?

13. He agrees to spare her brother, who has been condemned to death for fornication, if she will sleep with him. What Shakespeare play does this plot describe?

14. The earliest edition of Shakespeare's collected works was called what?

15. Which character in Shakespeare "lov'd not wisely but too well"?

16. Most of Shakespeare's plays were performed at this London theater. Name it.

17. What one Shakespeare play do these quotes come from?
    a) "Full fathom five thy father lies"
    b) "What's past is prologue"
    c) "We are such stuff as dreams are made on"

18. In what play by Shakespeare is Enobarbus a character?

19. Shakespeare wrote three plays about the same English monarch. Name them.

20. His "Queen Mab speech" is one of the most famous in all of Shakespeare. Name a) the character and b) the play in which he speaks this speech.

21. Disguised as a lawyer, she wins the case and saves the life of her husband's friend. Name a) this Shakespeare heroine and b) the play in which she appears.

22. In what Shakespeare plays do these quotes appear?
    a) "This blessed plot, this earth, this realm, this England"
    b) "Cry 'God for Harry! England and Saint George!' "
    c) "Heaven take my soul, and England keep my bones!"

23. In what Shakespeare play is the play-within-a-play *Pyramis and Thisbe* performed?

24. Much of this play takes place in the Forest of Arden. Name it.

25. Name the play in which all of these quotes occur:
   a) "False face must hide what the false heart doth know"
   b) "Something wicked this way comes"
   c) "Nothing in this life / Became him like the leaving it"

   Score_____

BRUSH UP YOUR SHAKESPEARE: ANSWERS

1. a) *Kiss Me Kate*, b) *The Taming of the Shrew*.
2. a) *The Tempest*, b) *Much Ado About Nothing*, c) *As You Like It*, d) *Twelfth Night*.
3. a) Cassius, b) *Julius Caesar*.
4. Goneril, Regan, and Cordelia.
5. a) *Henry IV, Part I*, b) *Henry IV, Part II*, c) *The Merry Wives of Windsor*.
6. *Hamlet*.
7. *The Two Gentlemen of Verona*.
8. Stratford-on-Avon.
9. a) revenge, b) jealousy, c) ambition, d) pride.
10. a) "Thou art more lovely and more temperate"
    b) "I summon up remembrance of things past"
    c) "So long lives this, and this gives life to thee"
    d) "I all alone beweep my outcast state"
11. a) *Antony and Cleopatra*, b) *Henry V*, c) *Richard III*.
12. Anne Hathaway.
13. *Measure for Measure*.
14. The First Folio.
15. Othello.
16. The Globe.
17. *The Tempest*.
18. *Antony and Cleopatra*.

19. *Henry VI, Parts I, II, and III.*
20. a) Mercutio, b) *Romeo and Juliet.*
21. a) Portia, b) *The Merchant of Venice.*
22. a) *Richard II*, b) *Henry V*, c) *King John.*
23. *A Midsummer Night's Dream.*
24. *As You Like It.*
25. *Macbeth.*

Common Knowledge
6

1. Who allegedly said, "We are not amused"?

2. How many spaces are there on these game boards?
    a) chess (or checkers)
    b) Monopoly
    c) Scrabble

3. True or false, Adlai E. Stevenson served as vice-president of the United States.

4. Alexander Calder made a) some sculptures that move and b) some that do not. What is each kind known as?

5. Who was the first Christian martyr and how did he die?

6. Match these ships with the wars in which they sank:
    a) *Maine*   a) World War I
    b) *Lusitania*   b) Spanish-American
    c) *Arizona*   War
    d) *Monitor*   c) Civil War
                           d) World War II

7. a) The star called Polaris is better known as what? b) In what constellation is it found?

8. Stephen Dedalus is the hero of this autobiographical novel. Name a) the book and b) its author.

9. What do these initials stand for?
   a) NOW
   b) NASA
   c) NAACP
   d) NSC

10. Alfred Nobel invented it in 1866. What was it?

11. What did a) the Eighteenth and b) the Nineteenth amendments to the U.S. Constitution, which both became law in 1920, accomplish?

12. The Russians launched the first one in 1957. What was it?

13. What is observed on these days?
   a) The second Sunday in May
   b) The first Monday in September
   c) The first Tuesday after the first Monday in November
   d) The first Sunday after the first full moon on or after the Spring Equinox

14. Under what pen name is Theodor Geisel better known?

15. What was the result of the Supreme Court decision of 1954 known as *Brown v. Board of Education of Topeka*?

16. Where is the National Baseball Hall of Fame located?

17. Which of these words does *not* belong with the others?
    a) hegemony
    b) autonomy
    c) sovereignty
    d) dominion

18. Members of what religion find spiritual wisdom in the *Bhagavad-Gita*?

19. What is a prairie schooner?

20. Bela Bartok, Aaron Copeland, and Paul Hindemith, among others, composed classical scores for this jazz musician. a) Who was he, and b) what instrument did he play?

21. In politics, what is meant by a dark horse?

22. How many—
    a) teaspoons in a tablespoon?
    b) cups in a pint?
    c) fluid ounces in a cup?
    d) tablespoons in a cup?

23. This Civil War illustrator for *Harper's Weekly* was later celebrated for his watercolors of the sea. Who was he?

24. On what denominations of U.S. currency are portraits of these people found?
    a) Andrew Jackson
    b) Benjamin Franklin
    c) Abraham Lincoln
    d) George Washington

24. What do Freer, Frick, and Fogg have in common?

Score_____

COMMON KNOWLEDGE 6:
ANSWERS

1. Queen Victoria.
2. a) 64, b) 40, c) 225.
3. True, but he was the grandfather of the twentieth-century Stevenson, and served under Grover Cleveland.
4. a) Mobiles, b) stabiles.
5. St. Stephen was stoned to death.
6. a) Spanish-American War, b) World War I, c) World War II, d) Civil War.
7. a) The North Star, b) the Little Dipper or Little Bear.
8. a) *A Portrait of the Artist as a Young Man* by b) James Joyce.
9. a) National Organization for Women, b) National Aeronautics and Space Administration, c) National Association for the Advancement of Colored People, d) National Security Council.
10. Dynamite.
11. a) The Eighteenth prohibited sale of alcohol, and b) the Nineteenth gave women the right to vote.
12. Sputnik I, the first man-made satellite.
13. a) Mother's Day, b) Labor Day, c) Election Day, d) Easter Sunday.
14. Dr. Seuss.
15. The Court declared racial segregation in schools unconstitutional.
16. Cooperstown, New York.
17. *Autonomy* implies independence, whereas the others refer to domination or control over others.
18. Hinduism.

19. A kind of covered wagon.
20. a) Benny Goodman, b) the clarinet.
21. A surprising choice to run for public office; one who is not an expected candidate.
22. a) 3, b) 2, c) 8, d) 16.
23. Winslow Homer.
24. a) $20, b) $100, c) $5, d) $1.
25. They are all renowned art museums.

Run for the Roses

1. Concerning the song "Everything's Coming Up Roses," name—
    a) the Broadway show it is from
    b) its composer
    c) the singer who introduced it

2. What is roseola better known as?

3. She won an Oscar as best supporting actress in this 1968 film. Name both a) movie and b) actress.

4. a) What actress originated the role of Serafina in Tennessee Williams's play *The Rose Tattoo*? b) What actress won an Oscar for her performance in the movie version?

5. a) The line "There's rosemary, that's for remembrance" comes from what play? b) What character speaks it?

6. What is a rosarium?

7. She worked in a factory when her man went off to war. Who was she?

8. It proved the key to deciphering Egyptian hieroglyphics. What was it called?

9. The Wars of the Roses were fought—
    a) in what country?
    b) in what century?
    c) between what two noble houses?

10. What film ends with the word "rosebud"?

11. What sporting event is known as "the run for the roses"?

12. Jeanette MacDonald and Nelson Eddy sang "Indian Love Call" in this movie. Name a) the film and b) the composer of the operetta on which it was based.

13. This a) matriarch was mother to b) a United States president, c) an attorney general and d) a senator. Name all four.

14. In what city is the Rose Bowl football game played?

15. Name these "rosy" sporting characters:
    a) a tarnished baseball star
    b) an Australian tennis ace
    c) a light heavyweight champion
    d) a football commissioner

16. a) Who wrote the play *Rosencrantz and Gildenstern Are Dead*, and b) from what play is his title a direct quote?

17. Who penned the following lines?
    a) "O, my Luve's like a red red rose
       That's newly sprung in June"
    b) "Rose is a rose is a rose is a rose"

c) " 'Tis the last rose of summer
Left blooming alone"

d) "The rainbow comes and goes,
And lovely is the rose"

18. St. Rose of Lima was the first. The first what?

19. Where would one find a rose window?

20. Who composed the opera *Der Rosenkavalier*?

21. a) What Shakespeare character speaks the line "A rose by any other name would smell as sweet," and b) to whom is it addressed?

22. A book, a movie, and a popular song all bear this "rosy" first-person title. What is it?

23. What is the meaning of the phrase *sub rosa*?

24. The words "They are not long" precede this poetic phrase that became a famous movie title. What is it?

25. This couple died on June 19, 1953. Who were they and why are they remembered?

Score_____

RUN FOR THE ROSES: ANSWERS

1. a) *Gypsy*, b) Jule Styne, c) Ethel Merman.
2. Measles.
3. a) *Rosemary's Baby*, b) Ruth Gordon.
4. a) Maureen Stapleton, b) Anna Magnani.
5. a) *Hamlet*, b) Ophelia.

6. A rose garden.

7. Rosie the Riveter.

8. The Rosetta Stone.

9. a) England, b) fifteenth, c) York and Lancaster.

10. *Citizen Kane*.

11. The Kentucky Derby.

12. a) *Rose Marie*, b) Rudolf Friml.

13. a) Rose Kennedy, b) John F. Kennedy, c) Robert Kennedy, d) Edward Kennedy.

14. Pasadena, California.

15. a) Pete Rose, b) Ken Rosewall, c) Maxie Rosenbloom, d) Pete Rozelle.

16. a) Tom Stoppard, b) *Hamlet*.

17. a) Robert Burns, b) Gertrude Stein, c) Thomas Moore, d) William Wordsworth.

18. The first canonized saint of the New World.

19. In a church.

20. Richard Strauss.

21. a) Juliet, b) Romeo.

22. *I Never Promised You a Rose Garden*.

23. In complete confidence and privacy.

24. *The Days of Wine and Roses*.

25. Julius and Ethel Rosenberg were executed for passing atomic secrets to Russia.

Q Is for Question

1. Match these places with the countries in which they are located:

a) Queensland	a) Canada
b) Quezon City	b) Ecuador
c) Quebec	c) Australia
d) Quito	d) Philippines

2. Quaker is a popular name for a member of what religious group?

3. Where, specifically, would you be if you found yourself on the Quai d'Orsay?

4. a) What activity are the letters QR, QKt, and QP associated with, and b) what do they stand for?

5. What is a quahog?

6. Define the following "quad" words:
   - a) quadroon
   - b) quadruped
   - c) quadrant
   - d) quadrille

7. What is the full name (including first and middle) of Vice-president Dan Quayle?

8. Allan Quartermain is the hero of what often filmed adventure story? Give a) title and b) author.

9. Real men don't eat this, according to the title of a humorous best-seller. What is it?

10. Would you find Queen Anne's lace—
       a) in a royal trousseau?
       b) in a meadow?
       c) in a greenhouse?
       d) in an antique shop?

11. This metallic structure is a common type of barracks or storage shed. Name it.

12. Who wrote these "quiet" novels?
       a) *The Quiet American*
       b) *All Quiet on the Western Front*
       c) *And Quiet Flows the Don*

13. Robert Taylor and Deborah Kerr starred in this epic movie based on the Henryk Sienkiewicz novel. Name it.

14. Muammar al Qadhafi is the president of what country?

15. The Marquis of Queensberry rules govern what sport?

16. Identify these fictional "Q" characters:
       a) a paranoid naval officer
       b) a TV medical examiner
       c) an impractical knight
       d) a hunchback

17. The most famous of these was named Dionne. What are they?

18. What is a quisling?

19. His guerrilla raiders were widely feared during the Civil War. Name him.

20. If you were down to your last quid in London, what would you have?

21. Name the instruments that typically comprise a string quartet.

22. What is the meaning of the phrase *on the Q.T.*?

23. Quickly, identify these ''Q'' words that may be found—
     a) in a thermometer
     b) in a swamp
     c) in a ballroom

24. James Joyce coined this word, which was later applied to elementary particles of matter. What is it?

25. Who wrote these ''quiet'' lines?
     a) ''The mass of men lead lives of quiet desperation''
     b) ''Thou still unravish'd bride of quietness''
     c) ''The holy time is quiet as a nun''
     d) ''Easy live and quiet die''

Score_____

Q IS FOR QUESTION: ANSWERS

1. a) Australia, b) Philippines, c) Canada, d) Ecuador.
2. Society of Friends.
3. On the south bank of the River Seine in Paris, France.

4. a) chess, b) queen's rook, queen's knight, queen's pawn.
5. A kind of clam.
6. a) Someone who is one-quarter black.
   b) A four-footed animal.
   c) One-quarter of a circle.
   d) A kind of square dance for four couples.
7. James Danforth Quayle.
8. a) *King Solomon's Mines*, b) H. Rider Haggard.
9. Quiche.
10. b) in a meadow.
11. Quonset hut.
12. a) Graham Greene, b) Erich Maria Remarque, c)
Mikhail Sholokhov.
13. *Quo Vadis?*
14. Libya.
15. Boxing.
16. a) Captain Queeg, b) Quincy, c) Don Quixote, d)
Quasimodo.
17. Quintuplets.
18. A traitor who sides with an invading enemy of his country.
19. William Clarke Quantrill.
20. One pound.
21. Two violins, a viola, and a cello.
22. In secret.
23. a) quicksilver (mercury), b) quicksand, c) quickstep.
24. Quark.
25. a) Henry David Thoreau, b) John Keats, c) William
Wordsworth, d) Sir Walter Scott.

Middle School

A number of celebrated people are usually identified by three full names: e.g., Franklin Delano Roosevelt. Each of the following questions lists three distinguishing *middle* names along with three professions. The trick is to provide the full names of these people and connect them with what they did or do.

1. a) Bel
   b) Eliot
   c) Washington

   a) botanist
   b) actress
   c) historian

2. a) Jacob
   b) Morrow
   c) Ford

   a) capitalist
   b) movie director
   c) author

3. a) Rice
   b) Alva
   c) Earl

   a) inventor
   b) actor
   c) author

4. a) Frederick
   b) Taylor
   c) Gurley

   a) composer
   b) publisher
   c) poet

5. a) Conan — a) mystery writer
   b) Stanley — b) mystery writer
   c) Roberts — c) mystery writer

6. a) Fenimore — a) author
   b) Rose — b) stripper
   c) Kenneth — c) economist

7. a) Hart — a) ornithologist
   b) Foster — b) statesman
   c) Tory — c) artist

8. a) Brinsley — a) actor
   b) Dee — b) playwright
   c) Bernard — c) playwright

9. a) Sebastian — a) general
   b) Armstrong — b) lyricist
   c) Jay — c) composer

10. a) Luther — a) author
    b) Randolph — b) civil rights leader
    c) Maria — c) publisher

11. a) Vincent — a) poet
    b) St. Vincent — b) clergyman
    c) Vincent — c) poet

12. a) Singer — a) actress
    b) Waldo — b) artist
    c) Tyler — c) author

13. a) Wilkes — a) jurist
    b) Gould — b) author
    c) Wendell — c) assassin

14. a) Maynard   a) economist
    b) Penn   b) conductor
    c) Tilson   c) author

15. a) Carlos   a) poet
    b) Butler   b) poet
    c) Cullen   c) poet

16. a) Steele   a) religious leader
    b) Baker   b) historian
    c) David   c) author

17. a) Paul   a) author
    b) Jennings   b) naval hero
    c) Louis   c) politician

18. a) Christian   a) poet
    b) Manley   b) composer
    c) Philip   c) author

19. a) Makepeace   a) author
    b) Singleton   b) singer
    c) Lee   c) artist

20. a) Ward   a) composer
    b) Scott   b) poet
    c) Amadeus   c) civil rights leader

21. a) Stuart   a) parks designer
    b) Wadsworth   b) poet
    c) Law   c) economist

22. a) Allan   a) poet
    b) Barrett   b) poet
    c) Bysshe   c) poet

23. a) Lloyd   a) architect
     b) Graham   b) author
     c) Beecher   c) inventor

24. a) Scott   a) composer
     b) Carlo   b) author
     c) Chandler   c) poet/patriot

25. a) Bashevis   a) poet
     b) Greenleaf   b) author
     c) Baxter   c) actress

Score_____

MIDDLE SCHOOL: ANSWERS

1. a) Barbara Bel Geddes, actress; b) Samuel Eliot Morrison, historian; c) George Washington Carver, botanist.
2. a) John Jacob Astor, capitalist; b) Anne Morrow Lindbergh, author; c) Francis Ford Coppola, movie director.
3. a) Edgar Rice Burroughs, author; b) Thomas Alva Edison, inventor; c) James Earl Jones, actor.
4. a) George Frederick Handel, composer; b) Samuel Taylor Coleridge, poet; c) Helen Gurley Brown, publisher.
5. a) Arthur Conan Doyle; b) Earle Stanley Gardner; c) Mary Roberts Rinehart.
6. a) James Fenimore Cooper, author; b) Gypsy Rose Lee, stripper; c) John Kenneth Galbraith, economist.
7. a) Thomas Hart Benton, artist; b) John Foster Dulles, statesman; c) Roger Tory Peterson, ornithologist.
8. a) Richard Brinsley Sheridan, playwright; b) Billy Dee Williams, actor; c) George Bernard Shaw, playwright.
9. a) Johan Sebastian Bach, composer; b) George Armstrong Custer, general; c) Alan Jay Lerner, lyricist.
10. a) Martin Luther King, Jr., civil rights leader;

b) William Randolph Hearst, publisher; c) Erich Maria Remarque, author.

11. a) Norman Vincent Peale, clergyman; b) Edna St. Vincent Millay, poet; c) Stephen Vincent Benet, poet.

12. a) John Singer Sargent, artist; b) Ralph Waldo Emerson, author; c) Mary Tyler Moore, actress.

13. a) John Wilkes Booth, assassin; b) James Gould Cozzens, author; c) Oliver Wendell Holmes, jurist.

14. a) John Maynard Keynes, economist; b) Robert Penn Warren, author; c) Michael Tilson Thomas, conductor.

15. a) William Carlos Williams; b) William Butler Yeats; c) William Cullen Bryant.

16. a) Henry Steele Commanger, historian; b) Mary Baker Eddy, religious leader; c) Henry David Thoreau, author.

17. a) John Paul Jones, naval hero; b) William Jennings Bryan, politician; c) Robert Louis Stevenson, author.

18. a) Hans Christian Andersen, author; b) Gerard Manley Hopkins, poet; c) John Philip Sousa, composer.

19. a) William Makepeace Thackery, author; b) John Singleton Copley, artist; c) Jerry Lee Lewis, singer.

20. a) Julia Ward Howe, poet; b) Coretta Scott King, civil rights leader; c) Wolfgang Amadeus Mozart, composer.

21. a) John Stuart Mill, philosopher; b) Henry Wadsworth Longfellow, poet; c) Frederick Law Olmsted, parks designer.

22. a) Edgar Allan Poe; b) Elizabeth Barrett Browning; c) Percy Bysshe Shelley.

23. a) Frank Lloyd Wright, architect; b) Alexander Graham Bell, inventor; c) Harriet Beecher Stowe, author.

24. a) Francis Scott Key, poet/patriot; b) Gian Carlo Menotti, composer; c) Joel Chandler Harris, author.

25. a) Isaac Bashevis Singer, author; b) John Greenleaf Whittier, poet; c) Meredith Baxter Birnie, actress.

Common Knowledge
7

1. Man meets fish, man catches fish, man loses fish. What literary work is thus described?

2. This charter of 1215 limited the power of the king. Name—
    a) the charter
    b) the king who signed it
    c) the place where it was signed

3. *Prague*, *Linz*, and *Jupiter* denote symphonies by what composer?

4. What is meant by Hobson's choice?

5. In a solar eclipse, does—
    a) the sun pass between the earth and the moon?
    b) the moon pass between the sun and the earth?
    c) the earth pass between the moon and the sun?

6. Sergeant William Brown of Connecticut received the first one in 1782. a) What was it, and b) who gave it to him?

7. The source of light in his paintings, of which only thirty-five are known, is often an open window. Name the artist.

8. a) In what war did the Green Mountain Boys play a role, and b) who was their leader?

9. What do these phrases mean in law?
   a) *noncompos mentis*
   b) *amicus curiae*
   c) *in loco parentis*

10. A phrase employing the name of this mythological hero is used to describe someone's weakest or most vulnerable point. What is the phrase?

11. Among his novels are *The Pioneers*, *The Pilot*, *The Prairie*, and *The Pathfinder*. Who wrote them?

12. More than three hundred thousand allied troops were evacuated from this French port city early in World War II. Name it.

13. What do these initials stand for?
   a) CIA
   b) FBI
   c) FDA
   d) HUD

14. General George Armstrong Custer met his fate near the banks of this river. Name it.

15. In what cities are these TV sitcoms set?
   a) "Mork and Mindy"
   b) "Designing Women"
   c) "The Mary Tyler Moore Show"
   d) "Happy Days"

16. In a 1946 speech in Fulton, Missouri, he coined the phrase "Iron Curtain." Who was he?

17. For what classic children's tale is L. Frank Baum best known?

18. a) Who founded the Society of Jesus, and b) what are its members called?

19. Which of these words does *not* belong with the others, and why?
    a) apathetic
    b) lethargic
    c) sanguine
    d) phlegmatic

20. Name the three yellow properties on a Monopoly board.

21. This congressional act of 1964 led to a great escalation of the Vietnam War. What was it called?

22. What is meant by the expression *whipping boy*?

23. When crossing the international date line from east to west, is a day gained or lost?

24. Connect these religions with their founders:
    a) Society of Friends   a) Joseph Smith
    b) Presbyterian   b) John Wesley
       Church   c) John Knox
    c) Methodist Church   d) George Fox
    d) Church of Jesus
       Christ of Latter-
       Day Saints

25. What rock group did Sid Vicious and Johnny Rotten belong to?

Score_____

COMMON KNOWLEDGE 7: ANSWERS

1. *The Old Man and the Sea* by Ernest Hemingway.
2. a) Magna Carta, b) King John of England, c) Runnymede.
3. Wolfgang Amadeus Mozart.
4. A choice without any alternatives, meaning no real choice at all.
5. b) The moon passes between the sun and the earth.
6. a) The first Purple Heart was awarded by b) George Washington.
7. Jan Vermeer.
8. a) The American Revolution, b) Ethan Allen.
9. a) mentally incompetent (to stand trial), b) friend of the court, c) in place of parents.
10. Achilles' heel.
11. James Fenimore Cooper.
12. Dunkirk.
13. a) Central Intelligence Agency, b) Federal Bureau of Investigation, c) Food and Drug Administration, d) [Department of] Housing and Urban Development.
14. Little Big Horn.
15. a) Boulder, Colorado, b) Atlanta, Georgia, c) Minneapolis, Minnesota, d) Milwaukee, Wisconsin.
16. Winston Churchill.
17. *The Wonderful Wizard of Oz*.
18. a) St. Ignatius of Loyola, b) Jesuits.
19. *Sanguine* means hopeful and confident; the others suggest a sluggish temperament.

20. Atlantic Avenue, Ventnor Avenue, Marvin Gardens.
21. The Gulf of Tonkin Resolution.
22. A scapegoat, or someone on whom blame and punishment are placed for another's fault.
23. A day is lost.
24. a) George Fox, b) John Knox, c) John Wesley, d) Joseph Smith.
25. The Sex Pistols.

Quoth the Raven

Who spoke or wrote the following lines?

1. "You can fool all of the people some of the time, and some of the people all of the time, but you can not fool all the people all of the time."

2. A cynic is ". . . a man who knows the price of everything and the value of nothing."

3. "I cannot forecast to you the action of Russia. It is a riddle, wrapped in a mystery inside an enigma."

4. "Give me chastity and continency—but not yet!"

5. "Patriotism is the last refuge of a scoundrel."

6. "I have not yet begun to fight."

7. "Let me assert my firm belief that the only thing we have to fear is fear itself."

8. "Work expands so as to fill the time available for its completion."

9. "Men seldom make passes / At girls who wear glasses."

10. "The grave's a fine and private place, / But none I think do there embrace."

11. "Political power grows out of the barrel of a gun."

12. "If this be treason, make the most of it."

13. "Extraordinary how potent cheap music is."

14. "We must indeed all hang together, or, most assuredly, we shall all hang separately."

15. "Home is the place where, when you have to go there, / They have to take you in."

16. "You can include me out."

17. "Religion is the opium of the people."

18. ". . . the only way to have a friend is to be one."

19. "If you can't stand the heat, get out of the kitchen."

20. A classic is ". . . something that everybody wants to have read and nobody wants to read."

21. "He who can, does. He who cannot teaches."

22. "The mass of men lead lives of quiet desperation."

23. "How sharper than a serpent's tooth it is / To have a thankless child!"

24. "These are the times that try men's souls."

25. "It is a truth universally acknowledged, that a single man in possession of a good fortune, must be in want of a wife."

Score_____

QUOTH THE RAVEN: ANSWERS

1. Abraham Lincoln.
2. Oscar Wilde.
3. Winston Churchill.
4. St. Augustine.
5. Samuel Johnson.
6. John Paul Jones.
7. Franklin D. Roosevelt.
8. C. Northcote Parkinson.
9. Dorothy Parker.
10. Andrew Marvell.
11. Mao Zedong
12. Patrick Henry.
13. Noel Coward.
14. Benjamin Franklin.
15. Robert Frost.
16. Samuel Goldwyn.
17. Karl Marx.
18. Ralph Waldo Emerson.
19. Harry S Truman.
20. Mark Twain.
21. George Bernard Shaw.
22. Henry David Thoreau.
23. William Shakespeare.
24. Tom Paine.
25. Jane Austen.

Music Hath Charms

1. Schubert, Dvorak, and Mahler all matched Beethoven in this department. What did they do?

2. a) Who composed the operas *Das Rheingold, Die Walkürie, Siegfried,* and *Die Götterdämmerung,* and b) under what name are they collectively known?

3. Name the operas (and their composers) in which the following groups of characters appear:
   a) Pooh-bah, Pish-tush, Pitti-sing
   b) Pamina, Papageno, Papagena
   c) Ping, Pang, Pong

4. This ballet caused a riot when performed in Paris in 1913. Name—
   a) the ballet
   b) its composer
   c) the impresario who presented it

5. Giuseppi Verdi composed three operas based on plays by Shakespeare, two of which are *Macbeth* and *Othello.* Name a) the third opera and b) the play that inspired it.

6. Connect these waltzes with their composers:

a)	*Waltz of the Flowers*	a)	Franz Lehar
		b)	Franz Liszt
b)	*Musetta's Waltz*	c)	Peter Ilyitch
c)	*Merry Widow Waltz*		Tchaikovsky
d)	*Mephisto Waltz*	d)	Giacomo Puccini

7. His twelve-tone system of composition revolutionized twentieth-century music. Name him.

8. She was jilted by Aristotle Onassis. Name this fiery diva.

9. This composer/conductor wrote the scores for the Broadway shows *On the Town*, *West Side Story*, and *Candide*. Who was he?

10. These performers were largely responsible for reviving their musical instruments in the twentieth century. Name their instruments:
    a) Wanda Landowska
    b) Pablo Casals
    c) Andres Segovia

11. Renata Tebaldi dubbed the singing for Sophia Loren in a movie version of what famous opera?

12. Who composed these works?
    a) *Enigma Variations*
    b) *Diabelli Variations*
    c) *Goldberg Variations*

13. This prolific composer of film scores also is the conductor of the Boston "Pops" Orchestra. What is his name?

14. Connect these conductors with the orchestra with which they are most closely associated:
  - a) Herbert Von Karajan
  - b) Arturo Toscaninni
  - c) Serge Koussevitzki
  - d) Leonard Bernstein
  - a) NBC Symphony
  - b) New York Philharmonic
  - c) Berlin Philharmonic
  - d) Boston Symphony

15. Arrange these tempo directions in order from slowest to fastest: *andante*, *allegro*, *largo*, *adagio*.

16. This jazz pianist/composer/conductor was once married to Mia Farrow. Name him.

17. A famous tenor and a famous soprano who frequently perform together were both born in the city of Modena, Italy. Who are they?

18. These sobriquets are applied to symphonies by what composers?
  - a) *Prague*
  - b) *Classical*
  - c) *Pastoral*
  - d) *New World*

19. Berlioz, Gounod, Tchaikovsky, and Prokofiev all composed works inspired by this play by Shakespeare. Which play is it?

20. W. S. Gilbert and Arthur Sullivan form one of the most famous teams in musical history. Which one wrote the music and which the words?

21. What are the four major instrument groups in a symphony orchestra?

22. To what composer did Robert Schumann refer when he wrote, "Hats off, gentlemen, a genius!"

23. Who wrote the following operas?
    a) *Don Carlos*
    b) *Don Giovanni*
    c) *Don Pasquale*

24. "Budapest," "Cleveland," and "Julliard" are examples of what kind of musical ensemble?

25. This musician was accorded a Broadway ticker-tape parade in 1958. a) Who is he, and b) what had he done to earn it?

Score_____

MUSIC HATH CHARMS: ANSWERS

1. They all wrote nine symphonies.
2. a) Richard Wagner, b) *Der Ring des Niebelungen* or the Ring Cycle.
3. a) *The Mikado* by Gilbert and Sullivan, b) *The Magic Flute* by Mozart, c) *Turandot* by Puccini.
4. a) *Le Sacre du Printemps* (*The Rite of Spring*), b) Igor Stravinsky, c) Sergei Diaghilev.
5. a) *Falstaff*, b) *The Merry Wives of Windsor*.
6. a) Tchaikovsky, b) Puccini, c) Lehar, d) Liszt.
7. Arnold Schoenberg.
8. Maria Callas.
9. Leonard Bernstein.
10. a) harpsichord, b) cello, c) guitar.

11. *Aida.*
12. a) Edward Elgar, b) Ludwig von Beethoven, c) Johan Sebastian Bach.
13. John Williams.
14. a) Berlin Philharmonic, b) NBC Symphony, c) Boston Symphony, d) New York Philharmonic.
15. *Largo, adagio, andante, allegro.*
16. André Previn.
17. Luciano Pavarotti and Mirella Freni.
18. a) Mozart, b) Prokofiev, c) Beethoven, d) Dvorak.
19. *Romeo and Juliet.*
20. Sullivan wrote the music, Gilbert wrote the words.
21. Strings, winds, brass, percussion.
22. Fredric Chopin.
23. a) Verdi, b) Mozart, c) Donizetti.
24. String quartet.
25. a) Van Cliburn b) won first prize in the International Tchaikovsky Piano Competition in Moscow.

Shades of Meaning

Select the words or phrases below that best define the **boldface** words in each sentence.

1. Blushing, she destroyed his **salacious** letter.
   a) rude
   b) obscene
   c) intimate
   d) offensive

2. The spies were condemned to die for their **perfidy**.
   a) blasphemy
   b) profanity
   c) treachery
   d) infidelity

3. His most **salient** feature was a wart on his nose.
   a) revolting
   b) obvious
   c) negative
   d) prominent

4. The speech was **laconic**, to say the least.
   - a) concise
   - b) preachy
   - c) boring
   - d) wordy

5. In **perfervid** prose, he poured out his heart to his lover.
   - a) rich
   - b) impassioned
   - c) erotic
   - d) purple

6. Ancient and **perdurable**, the pyramids filled her with wonder.
   - a) awesome
   - b) beautiful
   - c) everlasting
   - d) mysterious

7. The kids' **fractious** mood was getting on our nerves.
   - a) hostile
   - b) irritable
   - c) silly
   - d) boisterous

8. If rioting continues, **draconian** measures may be required.
   - a) unusual
   - b) significant
   - c) legal
   - d) severe

9. Her **agoraphobia** confined her to her home.
   - a) fear of people
   - b) fear of flying
   - c) fear of open spaces
   - d) fear of disease

10. As the storm gathered, they felt an **inchoate** sense of danger.
   - a) beginning
   - b) mounting
   - c) slight
   - d) frightening

11. He skewered his enemies with **mordant** wit.
   - a) vicious
   - b) caustic
   - c) clever
   - d) outrageous

12. The garlic had become **desiccated** after long storage.
   - a) pungent
   - b) spoiled
   - c) moldy
   - d) dehydrated

13. Sailors quaked in fear as the **behemoth** approached.
   - a) battleship
   - b) tidal wave
   - c) monster
   - d) shark

14. The senator was shouted down for his **iconoclastic** views.
   - a) old-fashioned
   - b) challenging
   - c) conservative
   - d) liberal

15. The teachers questioned their **laissez faire** approach to child-rearing.
   - a) permissive
   - b) indifferent
   - c) careless
   - d) distant

16. His services were required on a **quotidian** basis.
   a) punctual
   b) infrequent
   c) everyday
   d) quarterly

17. Their attorney's closing argument was particularly **sagacious**.
   a) argumentative
   b) learned
   c) witty
   d) shrewd

18. His **cognomen** was well known throughout the county.
   a) image
   b) surname
   c) reputation
   d) ancestry

19. Their attempt at reconciliation led only to further **imbroglios**.
   a) complications
   b) arguments
   c) regrets
   d) recriminations

20. Lost and confused, he stumbled through the **labyrinthian** forest.
   a) threatening
   b) darkening
   c) mazelike
   d) dense

21. His once happy bride had become a **termagant**.
   a) recluse
   b) drunk

22. The **vicissitudes** of life continued to baffle her.
    a) uncertainty
    b) unfairness
    c) unreasonableness
    d) unsavoriness

23. Would these strangers prove **inimical**?
    a) indifferent
    b) hostile
    c) friendly
    d) helpful

24. His exacting work left no room for **contretemps**.
    a) indecision
    b) vacations
    c) sloppiness
    d) blunders

25. The **baroque** decor reminded her of a museum.
    a) opulent
    b) imposing
    c) ornate
    d) heavyhanded

                                    Score_____

SHADES OF MEANING: ANSWERS

1. obscene.
2. treachery.
3. prominent.
4. concise.

5. impassioned.
6. everlasting.
7. irritable.
8. severe.
9. fear of open spaces.
10. beginning.
11. caustic.
12. dehydrated.
13. monster.
14. challenging.
15. permissive.
16. everyday.
17. shrewd.
18. surname.
19. complications.
20. mazelike.
21. shrew.
22. uncertainty.
23. hostile.
24. blunders.
25. ornate.

Common Knowledge
8

1. Comic strips and soup cans contributed to this 1960's art movement. What was it called?

2. Who created these fictional doctors?
   a) Dr. Jeckyll
   b) Dr. Faustus
   c) Dr. Doolittle
   d) Dr. Zhivago

3. Where can one find these words inscribed?
Proclaim liberty throughout all the land
unto all the inhabitants thereof.

4. The Viking 1 and Viking 2 spacecraft both achieved this feat in 1976. What was it?

5. Which of these words does *not* belong with the others, and why?
   a) lachrymose
   b) apathetic
   c) lugubrious
   d) dolorous

6. Name the four railroads on a Monopoly board.

7. The discoveries of this Austrian monk established the principles of genetic inheritance. Who was he?

8. The Inquisition forced him to recant his belief that the earth orbited the sun. Who was he?

9. What groups are these rock-and-roll performers most closely associated with?
        a) Roger Daltry
        b) Brian Jones
        c) Jerry Garcia
        d) Robert Plant

10. What is the difference between a) a diagnosis and b) a prognosis?

11. What did Rosa Parks do in 1955 to ensure her place in U.S. History?

12. If a young cat is a kitten, what are the young of these animals called?
        a) lion
        b) deer
        c) swan
        d) whale

13. His hair was his undoing, and his name was not Samson. Who was this Biblical character and what happened to him?

14. A satirical drawing that exaggerates the subject's features to make him or her look foolish is called what?

15. Rank these British peers in order from highest to lowest:

a) marquis
b) earl
c) duke
d) viscount

16. From a critical point of view, what one adjective best describes all of the following expressions: *past history*, *fuse together*, and *temporary reprieve*.

17. Who was called the Sun King?

18. In mathematics, what is the number 3.1416 called, and what is the meaning of the term?

19. Name the American novels and their authors in which these characters appear:
a) Dick Diver
b) Hester Prynne
c) Jake Barnes
d) Isabel Archer

20. This early World War II battle was waged entirely in the air. Name it.

21. What does the acronym AIDS stand for?

22. Who wrote the following lines?
a) "On the eighteenth of April in Seventy-five"
b) "Oh, to be in England now that April's there"
c) "Their flag to April's breeze unfurl'd"
d) "April is the cruelest month"

23. Where is Mt. Suribachi and what is it known for?

24. Which of these songs was *not* written by Stephen Foster?

a) "The Old Folks at Home"
b) "My Old Kentucky Home"
c) "Carry Me Back to Old Virginny"
d) "Old Black Joe"

25. The only U.S. president to be impeached was acquitted by the Senate. Who was he?

Score_____

COMMON KNOWLEDGE 8: ANSWERS

1. Pop art.
2. a) Robert Louis Stevenson, b) Christopher Marlowe, c) Hugh Lofting, d) Boris Pasternak.
3. On the Liberty Bell.
4. They landed on Mars.
5. *Apathetic* means indifferent, while the others all suggest deep sadness.
6. Pennsylvania, Short Line, B & O, and Reading.
7. Gregor Mendel.
8. Galileo Galilei.
9. a) The Who, b) The Rolling Stones, c) The Grateful Dead, d) Led Zeppelin.
10. a) A doctor's diagnosis identifies a disease, b) his prognosis predicts its course.
11. The refusal of this black woman to give up her seat on a bus to a white person in Selma, Alabama, became a milestone in the civil rights movement.
12. a) cub, b) fawn, c) cygnet, d) calf.
13. Absalom was slain when his luxuriant hair caught in the branches of a tree.
14. A caricature.
15. a) duke, b) marquis, c) earl, d) viscount.

16. Redundant
17. Louis XIV of France.
18. *Pi* is the ratio of the circumference of a circle to its diameter.
19. a) *Tender is the Night* by F. Scott Fitzgerald, b) *The Scarlet Letter* by Nathaniel Hawthorne, c) *The Sun Also Rises* by Ernest Hemingway, d) *The Portrait of a Lady* by Henry James.
20. The Battle of Britain.
21. Acquired Immune Deficiency Syndrome.
22. a) Henry Wadsworth Longfellow, b) Robert Browning, c) Ralph Waldo Emerson, d) T. S. Eliot.
23. The famous victorious flag-raising by the U.S. Marines on the island of Iwo Jima took place there during World War II.
24. c) "Carry Me Back to Old Virginny."
25. Andrew Johnson.

A Sense of Direction

1. What do the initials NATO stand for?

2. The Brooklyn Bridge spans this body of water. Name it.

3. The authors of the following works share a common sur-name. Who are they?
    a) *The Day of the Locust*
    b) *The Meaning of Treason*
    c) *The Shoes of the Fisherman*
    d) *Friendly Persuasion*

4. What are northern lights more formally known as?

5. Where is Poet's Corner located?

6. They are also known as the Antilles. What are they?

7. Roald Amundsen was a) the first to reach the one, and b) the first to navigate the other. What two things did he accomplish?

8. Who wrote the following works?
    a) *East of Eden*
    b) *Theophilus North*
    c) *Westward Ho!*
    d) *North and South*

9. "You can be sure" if your purchase bears this brand name. What is it?

10. Where would you be if you found yourself—
    a) on the West Bank?
    b) in the East End?
    c) on South Island?
    d) in Northern Territory?

11. With the possible exception of the Ponderosa, this ranks as TV's most famous ranch. Name—
    a) the ranch
    b) the state where it's located
    c) the TV family that owns it
    d) the show on which it is featured

12. What is a southpaw?

13. Who wrote *Northanger Abbey*?

14. In a northeaster, does the wind blow from the northeast to southwest or from southwest to northeast?

15. His inventions made photography available to the masses. Who was he?

16. Owen Wister's novel *The Virginian* is generally considered to be the first. The first what?

17. Match these movies with their female stars:
    a) *South Pacific*   a) Mitzi Gaynor
    b) *West Side Story*   b) Judy Garland
    c) *North by Northwest*   c) Natalie Wood
    d) *Easter Parade*   d) Eva Marie Saint

18. Name the capital cities of a) North Dakota, b) South Dakota, c) North Carolina, and d) South Carolina.

19. In addition to the four states cited in 18, above, one other state has a "directional" name. Name a) that state and b) *its* capital.

20. Where would one look for the Southern Cross?

21. The South African War is better known as what?

22. She called her autobiography *Goodness Had Nothing to Do with It*. Who was she?

23. Squire Western is a character in this famous novel. Name a) the novel and b) its author.

24. The Eastern Shore lies along what body of water?

25. Who wrote the following lines?
   a) "O for a beaker full of the warm South"
   b) "O wild West Wind, thou breath of Autumn's being"
   c) "Oh, East is East, and West is West, and never the twain shall meet"
   d) "The North Wind doth blow, and we shall have snow"

Score_____

A SENSE OF DIRECTION: ANSWERS

1. North Atlantic Treaty Organization.
2. The East River.

3. a) Nathaniel West, b) Rebecca West, c) Morris West, d) Jessamyn West.
4. *Aurora borealis*.
5. In Westminster Abbey.
6. The West Indies.
7. a) Reached the South Pole, and b) navigated the Northwest Passage.
8. a) John Steinbeck, b) Thornton Wilder, c) Charles Kingsley, d) John Jakes.
9. Westinghouse.
10. a) Jerusalem, b) London, c) New Zealand, d) Australia.
11. a) Southfork, b) Texas, c) the Ewings, d) *Dallas*.
12. A left-handed person.
13. Jane Austen.
14. From northeast to southwest.
15. George Eastman.
16. Western novel.
17. a) Mitzi Gaynor, b) Natalie Wood, c) Eva Marie Saint, d) Judy Garland.
18. a) Bismarck, b) Pierre, c) Raleigh, d) Columbia.
19. a) West Virginia, b) Charleston.
20. In the night sky below the equator: it is a constellation.
21. The Boer War.
22. Mae West.
23. a) *Tom Jones*, b) Henry Fielding.
24. Chesapeake Bay.
25. a) John Keats, b) Percy Bysshe Shelley, c) Rudyard Kipling, d) Anonymous.

The Building Trade

1. Where would you find these towers?
    a) The Eiffel Tower
    b) The Sears Tower
    c) The Leaning Tower
    d) The Twin Towers (World Trade Center)

2. a) Who played the title role in the movie *Mr. Blandings Builds His Dream House*, and b) who played *Mrs.* Blandings?

3. What famous structure includes the Hall of Mirrors?

4. Architect Frank Lloyd Wright gave this Welsh name to his homes in Wisconsin and Arizona. What is it?

5. This tomb, built by a grieving husband, is considered by many to be the most beautiful building in the world. Name it.

6. Who lived in these historic homes?
    a) Mount Vernon
    b) Monticello
    c) The Hermitage
    d) Hyde Park

7. Under construction for nearly a century, it will be the world's largest cathedral on completion. What and where is it?

8. The first of these was completed in Chicago in 1885. The first what?

9. What architect proclaimed that "less is more"?

10. Link these world-class hotels with the cities in which they are located:

   a) George V   a) New York
   b) Plaza   b) Paris
   c) Claridge's   c) Chicago
   d) Palmer House   d) London

11. Who wrote the play *The Master Builder*?

12. This bestselling novel featured architect Howard Roark as its hero. Name a) the novel, b) its author, and c) the actor who portrayed Roark in the movies.

13. Identify by name and location the largest sports arenas a) of the ancient world and b) of today's world.

14. This children's classic by Laura Ingalls Wilder became a long-running television series. Name it.

15. More than 1,400 miles long and up to thirty feet high, it was a wonder of ancient construction. What is it?

16. His epitaph reads (in Latin) "If you seek a monument, look about you." a) Who is he, and b) what is the monument you would see?

17. Among this architect's best-known works is his own "glass box house" in Connecticut. Who is he?

18. Identify these "house" movies:
   a) David Mamet wrote and directed it.
   b) Vincent Price starred in this early 3-Der.
   c) Edgar Allen Poe's classic tale inspired it.
   d) Sophia Loren played housekeeper to Cary Grant's kids in this one.

19. His dictum "form follows function" influenced Frank Lloyd Wright among other modern architects. Who was he?

20. Anne Boleyn, among others, met her fate in this landmark structure. Name it.

21. Who wrote these "house" books?
   a) *The House of the Dead*
   b) *The House of Mirth*
   c) *The House of the Seven Gables*
   d) *Bleak House*

22. Ferdinand de Lesseps is credited with building this marvel of nineteenth-century engineering. What is it?

23. The Golden Gate and the George Washington are examples of what type of bridge?

24. Built on the Acropolis in Athens, it served as a temple to the goddess Athena. What is it?

25. Connect these famous cathedrals with the places where they may be found:
   a) Notre Dame   a) Florence
   b) The Duomo   b) Paris
   c) St. Peter's   c) Venice
   d) St. Mark's   d) Rome

Score_____

140

THE BUILDING TRADE: ANSWERS

1. a) Paris, b) Chicago, c) Pisa, Italy, d) New York City.
2. a) Cary Grant, b) Myrna Loy.
3. The Palace of Versailles.
4. Taliesin.
5. The Taj Mahal.
6. a) George Washington, b) Thomas Jefferson, c) Andrew Jackson, d) Franklin D. Roosevelt.
7. The Cathedral of St. John the Divine in New York City.
8. Skyscraper.
9. Mies van der Rohe.
10. a) Paris, b) New York, c) London, d) Chicago.
11. Henrik Ibsen.
12. a) *The Fountainhead*, b) Ayn Rand, c) Gary Cooper.
13. a) The Colosseum in Rome, b) the Superdome in New Orleans.
14. *The Little House on the Prairie*.
15. The Great Wall of China.
16. a) Architect Sir Christopher Wren, b) St. Paul's Cathedral, London.
17. Philip Johnson.
18. a) *House of Games*, b) *House of Wax*, c) *House of Usher*, or *Fall of the House of Usher*, d) *Houseboat*.
19. Louis Sullivan.
20. The Tower of London.
21. a) Feodor Dostoevsky, b) Edith Wharton, c) Nathaniel Hawthorne, d) Charles Dickens.
22. The Suez Canal.
23. Suspension.
24. The Parthenon.
25. a) Paris, b) Florence, c) Rome, d) Venice.

The Good Book

1. His name is synonymous with great age. a) Who was he and b) how long does the Bible tell us he lived?

2. Their names jointly represent a seemingly unequal contest between strong and weak adversaries. a) Who were they and b) what was the outcome of their contest?

3. Thomas Mann wrote a) a novel and Andrew Lloyd Webber b) a musical about this Biblical character. Name the two works.

4. Who were the three offspring of Adam and Eve?

5. John Milton described him as "eyeless in Gaza" in this famous poem. Name it.

6. Identify these biblical characters:
    a) He dreamed of a ladder.
    b) Twin brother of (a).
    c) Mother of (a).
    d) Sisters, both married to (a).

7. She was wife of David and mother of Solomon. Name her.

8. This prophet's vision inspired the traditional Negro song "Dem Bones." Who was he?

9. Her courage in interceding with her husband, the King of Persia, prevented a massacre of Jews. Who was this celebrated biblical heroine?

10. Fill in the appropriate words in the following story:
An angel spoke to Moses out of a a) _____, telling him to lead the Israelites to a land flowing with b) _____ and _____. Their escape from Egypt is known as the c) _____. God sent them d) _____ to eat on their travels through the desert.

11. The name of this great-grandson of Noah has become synonymous with "hunter." Who was he?

12. Who played the title roles in these biblical epic films?
    a) *David and Bathsheba*
    b) *Samson and Delilah*
    c) *Solomon and Sheba*

13. In this film, covering the first twenty-two chapters of Genesis, John Huston directed himself. Name a) the role he played and b) the title of the film.

14. His name is applied to one whose very presence brings bad luck to his companions. Who is this biblical character?

15. "Thy love to me was wonderful, passing the love of women." a) Who is speaking of b) whom in this quotation.

16. Who composed the contemporary opera *Moses and Aaron*?

17. "Am I my brother's keeper?" a) Who said it b) to whom, and c) to whom did the speaker refer?

18. Who wrote the novels *Absalom, Absalom!* and *Go Down, Moses*?

19. She foretold Saul's defeat and death at the hands of the Philistines. Who was she?

20. To whom did the Lord speak in "a still, small voice"?

21. Explain what is wrong with the following sentences:
    a) Tempted by Satan, Eve first tasted the fruit of the Tree of Life.
    b) Moses and his brother Aaron led the Israelites across the Jordan into the Promised Land.
    c) Noah survived the Flood in his Arc of the Covenant.

22. Among his biblical oratorios are *Esther*, Israel in Egypt, and *Saul*. Who is the composer?

23. He directed two epic biblical films under the title *The Ten Commandments*. Who was he?

24. He refused to curse God despite great misfortunes. Who was this long-suffering biblical character?

25. A wanton woman might still be branded with this biblical name. What is it?

Score_____

THE GOOD BOOK: ANSWERS

1. a) Methuselah, b) 969 years.
2. a) David and Goliath, b) David slew Goliath.
3. a) *Joseph and His Brethren*, b) *Joseph and the Amazing Technicolor Dreamcoat*.
4. Cain, Abel, and Seth.
5. *Samson Agonistes*.
6. a) Jacob, b) Esau, c) Rebecca, d) Rachel and Leah.
7. Bathsheba.
8. Ezekiel.
9. Esther.
10. a) burning bush, b) milk and honey, c) Exodus, d) manna.
11. Nimrod.
12. a) Gregory Peck and Susan Hayward, b) Victor Mature and Hedy Lamar, c) Yul Brynner and Gina Lollobrigida.
13. a) Noah, b) *The Bible*.
14. Jonah.
15. a) David, b) Jonathan.
16. Arnold Schoenberg.
17. a) Cain, b) God, c) Abel.
18. William Faulkner.
19. The Witch of En-dor.
20. Elijah.
21. a) The fruit was from the Tree of Knowledge of Good and Evil; b) Moses and Aaron both died before reaching the Promised Land; c) the Arc of the Covenant was a boxlike container holding the Ten Commandments, not the ship that saved Noah.
22. George Frederick Handel.
23. Cecil B. DeMille.
24. Job.
25. Jezebel.

Common Knowledge
9

1. This TV series character went down with the *Titanic*. Who was she?

2. Louise Nevelson, George Segal, and David Smith are known for their what?

3. Where are the following located?
   a) Great Barrier Reef
   b) Great Bear Lake
   c) Great Smoky Mountains
   d) Great Salt Lake

4. *Kind of Blue* and *Sketches of Spain* are considered to be among his best record albums. Who is he?

5. This disciple was the "rock" upon which Jesus founded his Church. Name him.

6. What chemical elements do these symbols represent?
   a) Au
   b) Fe
   c) Ag
   d) Na

7. What is the significance of Sutter's Mill in U.S. history?

8. What are monarchs, sulfurs, and swallowtails?

9. Which of these words does *not* belong with the others, and why?
- a) jovial
- b) jocund
- c) jejune
- d) jubilant

10. Many residents of Pitcairn Island are descended from the survivors of this historical event. What is it?

11. Two months of the year were named for Roman leaders. Which ones?

12. What is meant by the expression to travel "by shank's mare"?

13. What cocktails would result from mixing these ingredients?
- a) vodka and Kahlua
- b) white wine and creme de cassis
- c) gin, vermouth, and pearl onion
- d) scotch and Drambuie

14. His Broadway musicals include *Company*, *Follies*, and *A Little Night Music*. Who is the composer/librettist?

15. The phrase "to meet one's Waterloo" comes from what historical event?

16. a) Where can one find the following words inscribed, and b) who wrote them?
   I lift my lamp beside the golden door!

17. He said, "I shall return," and he did. Who said it and under what circumstances?

18. This spin-off character from the TV series *All In the Family* had a maid on her own series who was later spun off into *her* series. Name—
    a) the character
    b) her maid
    c) the maid's series

19. Where would one go to find permafrost and what is it?

20. In the so-called "monkey trial" of 1925—
    a) who was the defendant?
    b) what was he charged with?
    c) who defended him?
    d) who prosecuted him?

21. This program of economic aid for the countries of Europe after World War II was named for its sponsor. What was it called and who proposed it?

22. He gave his name to the process of heating milk in order to destroy toxic bacteria. Name the man and the process.

23. Where would one find red giants and white dwarfs?

24. Connect these newspapers with the cities where they are published:
    a) *Observer*   a) Sacramento, CA
    b) *Bee*   b) Cleveland, OH
    c) *Plain Dealer*   c) St. Louis, MO
    d) *Post-Dispatch*   d) Charlotte, NC

25. Usually referred to as "the" soliloquy from Shakespeare's *Hamlet*, its opening line is among the most famous in all literature. Quote it.

Score_____

COMMON KNOWLEDGE 9: ANSWERS

1. Lady Marjorie Bellamy of "Upstairs, Downstairs."
2. Sculpture.
3. a) Off the northeast coast of Australia, b) northern Canada, c) southeastern U.S. on the North Carolina/Tennessee border, d) Utah.
4. Miles Davis.
5. St. Peter.
6. a) gold, b) iron, c) silver, d) sodium.
7. The discovery of gold nearby set off the California Gold Rush of 1849.
8. Butterflies.
9. All mean happy and upbeat except *jejune*, which means bland or insipid.
10. The mutiny on the HMS *Bounty*.
11. July for Julius Caesar, August for Augustus Caesar.
12. To walk.
13. a) Black Russian, b) Kir, c) Gibson, d) Rusty Nail.
14. Stephen Sondheim.
15. The defeat of Napoleon Bonaparte by the British at the Battle of Waterloo.
16. a) In the pedestal of the Statue of Liberty, b) Emma Lazarus.
17. General Douglas MacArthur, on leaving the Philippines to the Japanese during World War II.
18. a) Maude Findlay, b) Florida Evans, c) "Good Times."

149

19. Found in Arctic areas, it is deeply and permanently frozen soil.

20. a) John Scopes, b) teaching the theory of evolution, c) Clarence Darrow, d) William Jennings Bryan.

21. The Marshall Plan was proposed by General George C. Marshall.

22. Louis Pasteur invented the process of pasteurization.

23. In space. They are stars.

24. a) Charlotte *Observer*, b) Sacramento *Bee*, c) Cleveland *Plain Dealer*, d) St. Louis *Post-Dispatch*.

25. ''To be or not to be: that is the question.''

World Class

1. Canada's Nova Scotia, New Brunswick, and Prince Edward Island are known collectively as what?

2. If you had traveled with these explorers, on what continents would you most likely have found yourself?
   a) Leif Ericson
   b) David Livingston
   c) Richard E. Byrd
   d) Marco Polo

3. Ten states of the United States have two-name names: e.g., New York. Name the other nine.

4. What and where are Mauna Kea and Mauna Loa?

5. Name the five Great Lakes in geographic order from east to west.

6. If you were in these "port" cities, where would you be?
   a) Port of Spain
   b) Port Moresby
   c) Port Said
   d) Port-au-Prince

7. In what state is the geographic center a) of the forty-eight contiguous United States? b) Of the fifty states?

8. Name the capitals of these South American countries:
    a) Bolivia
    b) Uruguay
    c) Brazil
    d) Paraguay

9. What is the capital of Australia?

10. Connect these African nations with their former names:
    a) Zimbabwe   a) Belgian Congo
    b) Zambia   b) Southern Rhodesia
    c) Zaire   c) Northern Rhodesia

11. What is the largest inland body of water in the world?

12. Identify these cities by their nicknames:
    a) Windy City
    b) City of Angels
    c) Crescent City
    d) Twin Cities

13. What is the highest mountain in Africa?

14. What bodies of water are connected by these straits?
    a) Strait of Magellan
    b) Bering Strait
    c) Strait of Gibraltar

15. In what states of the United States are the two farther-most geographic points located?

16. What is the world's longest river?

17. Apart from Australia, which is considered a continent, what (in order) are the three largest islands in the world?

18. Angel Falls, the highest waterfall in the world, is found in what country?

19. Name the highest mountains—
   a) in the world
   b) in Europe
   c) in North America
   d) in the United States

20. Where is the lowest point in altitude in the United States?

21. In what states of the fifty United States do these geographical points occur?
   a) the easternmost
   b) the westernmost
   c) the northernmost
   d) the southernmost

22. The Mason-Dixon line forms the boundary between what two states?

23. The so-called volcanic "Ring of Fire" surrounds what body of water?

24. In what body of water is the Isle of Man located?

25. Which end of the Panama Canal is farther east, the Caribbean or the Pacific?

Score_____

WORLD CLASS: ANSWERS

1. The Maritime Provinces.
2. a) North America, b) Africa, c) Antarctica, d) Asia.
3. New Hampshire, New Jersey, New Mexico, North Carolina, North Dakota, South Carolina, South Dakota, West Virginia, Rhode Island.
4. Volcanoes in Hawaii.
5. Ontario, Erie, Huron, Michigan, Superior.
6. a) Trinidad and Tobago, b) Papua New Guinea, c) Egypt, d) Haiti.
7. a) Kansas, b) South Dakota.
8. a) La Paz, b) Montevideo, c) Brasilia, d) Asuncion.
9. Canberra.
10. a) Southern Rhodesia, b) Northern Rhodesia, c) Belgian Congo.
11. The Caspian Sea.
12. a) Chicago, b) Los Angeles, c) New Orleans, d) St. Paul and Minneapolis.
13. Mt. Kilimanjaro.
14. a) Atlantic and Pacific oceans, b) Arctic Ocean and Bering Sea, c) Atlantic Ocean and Mediterranean Sea.
15. Florida and Hawaii.
16. The Nile
17. a) Greenland, b) New Guinea, c) Borneo.
18. Venezuela.
19. a) Mt. Everest, b) Mont Blanc, c) Mt. McKinley, d) Mt. Whitney.
20. Death Valley, California.
21. a) Maine, b) Alaska, c) Alaska, d) Hawaii.
22. Pennsylvania and Maryland.
23. Pacific Ocean.
24. Irish Sea.
25. The Pacific.

That's Entertainment

1. Name the Broadway musicals that were adapted from these nonmusical works:
    a) *The Matchmaker* by Thornton Wilder
    b) *Berlin Stories* by Christopher Isherwood
    c) *Liliom* by Ferenc Molnar
    d) *Don Quixote* by Miguel de Cervantes

2. Megalon and Mothra have been among his archenemies. Whose?

3. Johnny Weissmuller was the foremost interpreter of this movie role. Name it.

4. Complete these comic TV pairings:
    a) Laverne and—
    b) Rowan and—
    c) Mork and—
    d) Kate and—

5. What actor played both Buffalo Bill and ''Slap'' Maxwell on television?

6. Sid Caesar, Imogene Coca, Carl Reiner, and Howard Morris sparked this 1950s TV variety show. What was it?

7. The "voices" of cartoon characters Mr. Magoo and Bugs Bunny were both silenced in July, 1989. Who were they?

8. Jessica Tandy played her on the stage, Vivian Leigh in the movies. Name a) this Tennessee Williams character and b) the play in which she appears.

9. What composers' lives were portrayed in these films?
    a) *Night and Day*
    b) *Words and Music*
    c) *Rhapsody in Blue*

10. His ragtime music graced the 1973 movie *The Sting*. Who was he?

11. Ethel Merman starred as this character in the Broadway musical, Betty Hutton in the movie version. Name—
    a) the character
    b) the show
    c) the composer

12. His movie scores included *The Wizard of Oz*. Who was this composer?

13. This TV series's principal address was 165 Eaton Place. Name a) the show and b) the family who lived there.

14. The following pairs of actors all played in different versions of the same movie. What is its title?
    a) Janet Gaynor and Fredric March
    b) Judy Garland and James Mason
    c) Barbra Streisand and Kris Kristofferson

15. The Hortons of Salem have been mainstays of this soap opera from its inception. What is it?

16. Name the jazz musicians who are known by these nicknames, and match them with the instruments they play:
    a) Fats   a) trumpet
    b) Dizzie   b) saxophone
    c) Cannonball   c) clarinet
    d) Woody   d) piano

17. What was the name of the detective agency on TV's "Moonlighting"?

18. Another singer wrote the lyrics to this virtual theme song for Frank Sinatra. Name a) the singer and b) the song.

19. Identify these country singers:
    a) She goes "walkin' after midnight."
    b) She "stands by her man."
    c) "All [his] rowdy friends have settled down."
    d) Lucille "picked a fine time to leave [him]."

20. Where might one have seen the Flying Wallendas?

21. The title of this classic musical denotes a vanished venue of popular entertainment. Identify—
    a) the show
    b) its composer
    c) its librettist
    d) the author of the book

22. Who wrote the scores for the shows *Guys and Dolls*, *The Most Happy Fella*, and *How to Succeed in Business Without Really Trying*?

23. DeForest Kelley, James Doohan, and Walter Koenig are

among the supporting repertory players in this popular TV and movie series. Name it.

24. Who is known as the Divine Miss M?

25. These Olympic gold medalists of 1984 revolutionized the art of ice dancing. Who are they?

Score_____

THAT'S ENTERTAINMENT: ANSWERS

1. a) *Hello, Dolly*, b) *Cabaret*, c) *Carousel*, d) *Man of La Mancha*.
2. Godzilla's.
3. Tarzan.
4. a) Shirley, b) Martin, c) Mindy, d) Allie.
5. Dabney Coleman.
6. "Your Show of Shows."
7. a) Jim Backus (Magoo), b) Mel Blanc (Bugs).
8. a) Blanche Dubois, b) *A Streetcar Named Desire*.
9. a) Cole Porter, b) Richard Rodgers and Lorenz Hart, c) George Gershwin.
10. Scott Joplin.
11. a) Annie Oakley, b) *Annie Get Your Gun*, c) *Irving Berlin*.
12. Harold Arlen.
13. a) "Upstairs, Downstairs," b) the Bellamys.
14. *A Star Is Born*.
15. "Days of Our Lives."
16. a) Fats Waller, piano, b) Dizzie Gillespie, trumpet, c) Cannonball Adderly, saxophone, d) Woody Herman, clarinet.
17. Blue Moon Investigations.
18. a) Paul Anka, b) "My Way."

19. a) Patsy Cline, b) Tammy Wynette, c) Hank Williams, Jr., d) Kenny Rogers.
20. At the circus.
21. a) *Show Boat*, b) Jerome Kern, c) Oscar Hammerstein II, d) Edna Ferber.
22. Frank Loesser.
23. *Star Trek*.
24. Bette Midler.
25. Jayne Torvil and Christopher Dean.

Kiddie Korner

1. Identify these nursery rhyme Jacks:
   a) He suffered head trauma.
   b) He watched his cholesterol.
   c) His table manners were lacking.
   d) He was kind to cats.

2. Who wrote *The Wind in the Willows*?

3. a) In what story does Ichabod Crane appear? b) Who
wrote it?

4. Name a) title and b) author of the children's classic that
includes the ballads "Jabberwocky" and "The Walrus and
the Carpenter."

5. Identify these fictional "little" people:
   a) Amy, Jo, Meg, and Beth
   b) Sandy's mistress
   c) Heir to an earldom
   d) A thoughtful granddaughter

6. In the nursery rhyme "Sing a Song of Sixpence," what
were a) the king, b) the queen and c) the maid doing?

7. This beloved story is subtitled *The Autobiography of a Horse*. Name a) title and b) author.

8. Much of this adventurous tale takes place on the schooner *Hispaniola*. Name—
      a) the book
      b) the author
      c) the hero
      d) the villain

9. In what tale of the Arabian Nights does the phrase "open sesame" figure?

10. Sir John Tenniel is best remembered as the illustrator of this classic children's tale. Name it.

11. After our hero and his pal witness a murder, his conscience demands he tell the truth to save an innocent life, even though he and his girlfriend are in jeopardy from the real killer. Identify this story by a) title and author, and name b) the hero's pal, c) his girlfriend, and d) the killer.

12. In this story, a young elephant visits the banks of the "great, grey-green, greasy Limpopo River." Name a) the title of the book in which this story appears and b) its author, and c) tell what happened to the elephant.

13. Among his best-known stories are "The Little Mermaid" and "The Ugly Duckling." Who is the author?

14. Who is Babar's wife?

15. For what character is author P. L. Travers best remembered?

16. Who wrote the original stories on which these Walt Disney movies were based?
   a) *Bambi*
   b) *Pinocchio*
   c) *Song of the South*

17. In the fairy tale, how did the shoemaker reward the elves who made shoes for him?

18. In what fairy tale does the title character pose as the Marquis of Carabas?

19. E. B. White wrote three classic children's books. Name them.

20. In the one, a domestic dog reverts to nature; in the other, a wild dog is tamed. Name a) b) the two novels and c) their author.

21. Who wrote and illustrated *Where the Wild Things Are*?

22. In the Mother Goose rhymes—
   a) How much wool did the black sheep have?
   b) What time was it when the mouse ran down the clock?
   c) Who were the three men in the tub?
   d) Why did the pussy cat go to London?

23. This fairy-tale opera, often performed at Christmastime, is based on a story from the Brothers Grimm. Name a) the opera and b) its composer.

24. Among the many series of books he launched are the *Hardy Boys* and the *Nancy Drew* mysteries. Name this prolific author/publisher of books for young people.

25. Swiss authors Johanna Spyri and Johann Wyss each wrote an enduring and often filmed children's classic. Name a) the Spyri book and b) the Wyss book.

Score_____

KIDDIE KORNER: ANSWERS

1. a) Jack of "Jack and Jill," b) Jack Spratt, c) Jack Horner, d) Jack Stout.
2. Kenneth Grahame.
3. a) "The Legend of Sleepy Hollow," b) Washington Irving.
4. a) *Through the Looking Glass*, b) Lewis Carroll.
5. a) Louisa May Alcott's *Little Women*, b) Little Orphan Annie, c) Little Lord Fauntleroy, d) Little Red Ridinghood.
6. a) counting money, b) eating bread and honey, c) hanging out the clothes.
7. a) *Black Beauty*, b) Anna Sewell.
8. a) *Treasure Island*, b) Robert Louis Stevenson, c) Jim Hawkins, d) Long John Silver.
9. *Ali Baba and the Forty Thieves*.
10. *Alice's Adventures in Wonderland*.
11. a) *Tom Sawyer* by Mark Twain, b) Huckleberry Finn, c) Becky Thatcher, d) Injun Joe.
12. a) *Just So Stories*, b) Rudyard Kipling, c) the elephant's nose is stretched into a trunk by a crocodile.
13. Hans Christian Andersen.
14. Celeste.
15. Mary Poppins.
16. a) Felix Salten, b) Carlo Collodi, c) Joel Chandler Harris.
17. He and his wife sewed clothes for them because the elves were naked.
18. *Puss in Boots*.

19. a) *Stuart Little*, b) *Charlotte's Web*, c) *The Trumpet of the Swan*.
20. a) *The Call of the Wild*, b) *White Fang*, c) Jack London.
21. Maurice Sendak.
22. a) three bags full; b) the clock struck one; c) the butcher, the baker, the candlestick-maker; d) to visit the queen.
23. a) *Hansel and Gretel*, b) Englebert Humperdinck.
24. Edward L. Stratemeyer.
25. a) *Heidi*, b) *Swiss Family Robinson*.

Common Knowledge
10

1. Florence Ballard, Mary Wilson, and Diana Ross were collectively known as what?

2. In what works by Charles Dickens do these characters appear?
   - a) the Artful Dodger
   - b) Uriah Heap
   - c) Miss Havisham
   - d) Madame Defarge

3. What does a Wasserman test test for?

4. Who said, "The world must be made safe for democracy"?

5. Legend has it that he "fiddled while Rome burned." Who was he?

6. What are intense tropical storms called over these waters?
   - a) Atlantic Ocean
   - b) Pacific Ocean
   - c) Indian Ocean

7. What are a) the name and b) the color of Paul Bunyan's ox?

8. What is meant by a *deus ex machina*?

9. What do these initials stand for?
    a) VFW
    b) EPA
    c) ICBM
    d) GOP

10. Name a) the story and b) its author in which a man remains young and handsome while his portrait reflects his true age and corruption.

11. What two empires opposed each other in the Punic Wars?

12. The paintings of his "blue" and "rose" periods are highly prized. Who was he?

13. Which states are known by these nicknames?
    a) Hawkeye State
    b) Sunflower State
    c) Show-Me State
    d) Buckeye State

14. What is meant by a devil's advocate?

15. Lintel, buttress, and pediment are terms used in what field?

16. Their creator also provided the voice for one of the major Muppet characters. Name a) the creator and b) the character.

17. What units of measure define the following:
    a) 43,560 square feet
    b) 500 sheets of paper
    c) 12 dozen (of anything)
    d) 5,880,000,000,000 miles

18. Lady Caroline Lamb called him "Mad, bad, and dangerous to know." To whom was she referring?

19. This mythical, many-lived bird is a symbol of immortality. Name it.

20. Which of these words does *not* belong with the others, and why?
      a) financial
      b) monetary
      c) fiscal
      d) impecunious

21. What is a writ of *habeus corpus*?

22. What foreign phrase is used to describe the feeling that one has previously been in a place one is, in fact, experiencing for the first time?

23. Offered a choice, the crowd chose freedom for this criminal rather than for Jesus. What was his name?

24. Link these Zodiac signs with their identifying symbols:
      a) Aries   a) Goat
      b) Cancer   b) Ram
      c) Libra   c) Scales
      d) Capricorn   d) Crab

25. Aside from the principalities of Monaco and Andorra, name the six countries that share borders with France.

Score_____

COMMON KNOWLEDGE 10: ANSWERS

1. The Supremes.
2. a) *Oliver Twist*, b) *David Copperfield*, c) *Great Expectations*, d) *A Tale of Two Cities*.

3. Syphilis.

4. Woodrow Wilson.

5. The emperor Nero.

6. a) hurricane, b) typhoon, c) cyclone.

7. a) Babe, b) blue.

8. An outside theatrical device created by a playwright to arbitrarily resolve his characters' dilemmas.

9. a) Veterans of Foreign Wars, b) Environmental Protection Agency, c) Intercontinental Ballistic Missile, d) Grand Old Party.

10. a) *The Picture of Dorian Gray* by b) Oscar Wilde.

11. Rome and Carthage.

12. Pablo Picasso.

13. a) Iowa, b) Kansas, c) Missouri, d) Ohio.

14. One who deliberately puts forth all the negative points of an argument in order to achieve a fair decision.

15. Architecture.

16. a) Jim Henson, b) Kermit the Frog.

17. a) acre, b) ream, c) gross, d) light year.

18. Lord Byron.

19. The phoenix.

20. All have reference to money, but *impecunious* means *without* money.

21. A judicial order requiring the physical appearance of a prisoner in court to determine whether he or she has been legally imprisoned.

22. *déjà vu*.

23. Barabbas.

24. a) Ram, b) Crab, c) Scales, d) Goat.

25. Belgium, Luxembourg, West Germany, Switzerland, Italy, and Spain.

Double Trouble

Complete these famous pairings. (Score one-half point for each correct answer.)

1. Samson and—

2. Currier and—

3. Burns and—

4. Barnum and—

5. Calvin and—

6. Romeo and—

7. Scylla and—

8. Martin and—

9. Sacco and—

10. Simon and—

11. Penn and—

12. Torvil and—

13. Tom and—

14. Gilbert and—

15. Jekyll and—

16. Flatt and—

17. Dun and—

18. Lewis and—

19. Romulus and—

20. Adam and—

21. Rosencrantz and—

22. Dido and—

23. Ashford and—

24. Bob and—

25. Heloise and—

26. Rodgers and—

27. Tracy and—

28. Jack and—

29. Kaufman and—

30. Cheech and—

31. Fred and—

32. Troilus and—

33. Orville and—

34. Antony and—

35. Barnes and—

36. Amos and—

37. Bonnie and—

38. Porgy and—

39. Dick and—

40. Cagney and—

41. Sonny and—

42. Beatrice and—

43. Castor and—

44. Ozzie and—

45. Laurel and—

46. Cain and—

47. Ken and—

48. Lerner and—

49. Tristan and—

50. Abbott and—

Score_____

DOUBLE TROUBLE: ANSWERS

1. Delilah
2. Ives
3. Allen
4. Bailey
5. Hobbes
6. Juliet
7. Charybdis
8. Lewis
9. Vanzetti
10. Garfunkel (or Schuster)
11. Teller
12. Dean
13. Jerry
14. Sullivan
15. Hyde
16. Scruggs
17. Bradstreet
18. Clarke
19. Remus
20. Eve
21. Gildenstern
22. Aeneas
23. Simpson
24. Ray
25. Abelard
26. Hammerstein (or Hart)
27. Hepburn
28. Jill
29. Hart
30. Chong
31. Ginger
32. Cressida
33. Wilbur
34. Cleopatra
35. Noble
36. Andy
37. Clyde
38. Bess
39. Jane
40. Lacey
41. Cher
42. Benedick
43. Pollux
44. Harriett
45. Hardy
46. Abel
47. Barbie
48. Loewe
49. Isolde
50. Costello

Triple Threat

1. What are the names of—
   a) the Three Wisemen?
   b) the Three Musketeers?
   c) the Three Stooges?

2. What three rivers converge at Pittsburgh, Pennsylvania?

3. Who were known as the Big Three during World War II?

4. What popular name is applied to Beethoven's Third Symphony?

5. This Berthold Brecht/Kurt Weill musical play was revived on Broadway in 1989. Name—
   a) the musical
   b) its rock-and-roll star
   c) the character he played

6. Who wrote the play *The Three Sisters*?

7. Name the three ships of Christopher Columbus.

8. Who composed these musical works?
    a) *The Three-Cornered Hat*
    b) *Four Saints in Three Acts*
    c) *The Love for Three Oranges*

9. Name Donald Duck's three nephews.

10. What happened to the three blind mice of nursery rhyme fame?

11. In baseball, what is a three-bagger?

12. What dance is based on three-quarter time rhythm?

13. Identify these movies:
    a) Woman struggles with multiple personalities
    b) Women wish for romance in Rome
    c) Woman survives Japanese prison camp
    d) Women wonder which one's husband is cheating

14. Name the three holy children of the Old Testament who were cast by Nebuchadnezzar into the fiery furnace.

15. What three musical instruments comprise a piano trio?

16. a) Where is Three Mile Island, and b) why is it important?

17. What three comic actors starred in the 1986 film *¡Three Amigos!*?

18. Identify these TV series:
    a) John Ritter starred in it
    b) Fred MacMurray starred in it
    c) John Ritter starred in it

19. What are the three R's?

20. What is a *ménage à trois*?

21. What is a tricorn?

22. Name—
   a) the three primary colors
   b) the three natural kingdoms
   c) the three parts of the Trinity
   d) the three Christian graces

23. Who wrote the book *Three Lives*?

24. Outside of a zoo, where would you find a three-toed sloth?

25. Define an isosceles triangle.

Score_____

TRIPLE THREAT: ANSWERS

1. a) Gaspar, Melchior, Balthazar; b) Athos, Porthos, Aramis; c) Larry, Moe, Curly.
2. The Allegheny, Monongahela, and Ohio rivers.
3. Franklin D. Roosevelt, Winston Churchill, and Joseph Stalin.
4. *Eroica*.
5. a) *The Three-Penny Opera*, b) Sting, c) Mack the Knife.
6. Anton Chekhov.
7. *Nina, Pinta, Santa Maria*.
8. a) Manuel de Falla, b) Virgil Thomson, c) Sergei Prokofiev.
9. Huey, Dewey, Louis.

10. The farmer's wife cut off their tails with a carving knife.
11. A three-base hit, or triple.
12. The waltz.
13. a) *The Three Faces of Eve*, b) *Three Coins in the Fountain*, c) *Three Came Home*, d) *A Letter to Three Wives*.
14. Shadrach, Meshach, Abed-nego.
15. Piano, violin, cello.
16. a) Pennsylvania. b) It was the site of the worst nuclear accident in U.S. history.
17. Steve Martin, Chevy Chase, Martin Short.
18. a) *Three's Company*, b) *My Three Sons*, c) *Three's a Crowd*.
19. Reading, 'riting, 'rithmetic.
20. A three-sided relationship in which a man and two women or a woman and two men live together under the same roof.
21. A three-cornered hat.
22. a) red, blue, yellow; b) animal, vegetable, mineral; c) Father, Son, Holy Ghost (or Spirit); d) faith, hope, charity.
23. Gertrude Stein.
24. In a tree in the tropical forests of South America.
25. One that has two sides of equal length.

Lucky Sevens

1. What city is renowned for its seven hills?

2. Name the seven dwarfs from Walt Disney's *Snow White and the Seven Dwarfs*.

3. The mythological daughters of Atlas were placed in the heavens to form this cluster of seven stars. What is it called?

4. Name the Seven Deadly Sins.

5. Who was the seventh president of the United States?

6. Who wrote the following literary works?
   a) *The House of the Seven Gables*
   b) *Seventeen*
   c) *Seven Against Thebes*
   d) *Seven Pillars of Wisdom*

7. Concerning King Edward VII of England—
   a) Whom did he succeed to the throne?
   b) What was their relationship?
   c) By what nickname was he known?

8. Who wrote "Morning's at seven . . . all's right with the world!"?

9. Name at least three of the Seven Wonders of the Ancient World.

10. What are the Roman numerals for the numbers a) 7, b) 70, c) 700?

11. Seven-card stud is a variation of what card game?

12. This Christian sect observes its sabbath on Saturday. Name it.

13. Of what number is 7 the square root?

14. Who directed these "seven" movies?
   a) *The Seventh Seal*
   b) *The Seven Samurai*
   c) *Seven Beauties*
   d) *Seven Days in May*

15. The European Seven Years' War was known by what name on the North American continent?

16. A musical composition for seven instruments is known as what?

17. This 1954 movie has two "sevens" in its title. Name it.

18. President Franklin Roosevelt described it as a "date which will live in infamy." a) What was the date and b) what happened on it?

19. A famous detective encountered a famous psychiatrist in

this 1976 thriller. Name a) the detective, b) the psychiatrist, and c) the movie.

20. Identify these "seven" names and phrases:
    a) a convenience store
    b) the world's oceans
    c) a soft drink
    d) a state of bliss

21. This address was the title of a popular 1960s television detective series. Name it.

22. What right is protected by the seventh amendment to the United States Constitution?

23. New York City's Seventh Avenue is noted for what business?

24. What city claims the 76ers basketball team?

25. According to Genesis, what did God do on the seventh day of creation?

Score_____

LUCKY SEVENS: ANSWERS

1. Rome.
2. Doc, Dopey, Sneezy, Happy, Grumpy, Bashful, and Sleepy.
3. The Pleiades.
4. Pride, greed, lust, anger, gluttony, envy, and sloth.
5. Andrew Jackson.
6. a) Nathaniel Hawthorne, b) Booth Tarkington, c) Aeschylus, d) T. E. Lawrence (of Arabia).

7. a) Queen Victoria, b) mother/son, c) Bertie.

8. Robert Browning.

9. The Pyramids of Egypt, the Hanging Gardens of Babylon, the statue of Zeus at Olympia, the Pharos (lighthouse) at Alexandria, the temple of Artemis at Ephesus, the Colossus of Rhodes, the Mausoleum at Halicarnassus.

10. a) VII, b) LXX, d) DCC.

11. Poker.

12. Seventh-Day Adventists.

13. 49.

14. a) Ingmar Bergman, b) Akira Kurosawa, c) Lina Wertmuller, d) John Frankenheimer.

15. The French and Indian Wars.

16. Septet.

17. *Seven Brides for Seven Brothers*.

18. a) December 7, 1941; b) the Japanese attacked the U.S. naval base at Pearl Harbor, Hawaii.

19. a) Sherlock Holmes, b) Sigmund Freud, c) *The Seven Percent Solution*.

20. a) 7-Eleven, b) the Seven Seas, c) 7-UP, d) seventh heaven.

21. *77 Sunset Strip*.

22. The right to trial by jury in civil suits.

23. Design or garment business.

24. Philadelphia, Pennsylvania.

25. He rested.